"Don't you realize that you're asking for trouble?

"If I stay in this tent now, I intend to kiss every inch of your body slowly and then order you to undress me and do the same to me. Because if I'm going to have you at all, Caroline Faircroft, I'm going to have you until I'm completely sated with you. Now do you understand?"

"Yes," she admitted huskily.

"And do you want me to go?"

"No."

ANGELA DEVINE grew up in Tasmania, surrounded by forests, mountains and wild seas—it's no wonder she's not a fan of big cities. Before taking up writing, she worked as a teacher, librarian and university lecturer. As a young mother and Ph.D. student, she read romance fiction for enjoyment and later decided it would be even more fun to write. Angela is married with four children, loves chocolate and Twinings tea and hates to iron. Her current hobbies include gardening, bushwalking, traveling and listening to classical music.

Books by Angela Devine

HARLEQUIN PRESENTS
1538—WIFE FOR A NIGHT

ANGELA DEVINE

Seed of the Fire Lily

Harlequin Books

TORONTO • NEW YORK • LONDON
AMSTERDAM • PARIS • SYDNEY • HAMBURG
STOCKHOLM • ATHENS • TOKYO • MILAN
MADRID • WARSAW • BUDAPEST • AUCKLAND

ISBN 0-373-11621-7

SEED OF THE FIRE LILY

Copyright © 1992 by Angela Devine.

Printed in U.S.A.

CHAPTER ONE

THE sunlight was so bright that it was almost blinding. Caroline braked cautiously and the four-wheel-drive vehicle lurched to a halt under a huge, spreading gum tree. Gratefully she wrenched the door open and climbed out, but if anything it was even hotter outside. Although it was late July and supposedly winter, the air descended on her like a blowtorch.

'This is worse than the cactus house at Kew Gardens!' she muttered ruefully, running her fingers through her damp brown hair. 'Definitely time for a drink and a clean T-shirt.'

Opening the hatchback of the jeep, she stared thoughtfully at the neatly packed bags and boxes inside. Mint-green this time, she decided, to match her shorts. After all, just because she was in the Australian outback with no other human being for miles around, there was no need to let her standards slip. Yet as she peeled the sticky T-shirt off her slim white body, she caught herself glancing furtively around. But the only living things to observe her were a trail of large black ants, swarming busily around a hole in the red earth. With a spurt of laughter at her own foolishness, Caroline relaxed. Picking up a water canteen, she unscrewed the top and poured the contents over her head. The water felt unexpectedly cold, and she gasped and sluiced herself as it ran in rivulets over her small, firm breasts. Snatching up a towel, she briskly dried her hair and pulled on the clean T-shirt.

'That felt good! Now, a drink and something to eat, but first I must comb my hair. It feels like wet rope.'

It only took her a moment to set up the folding chair and table. Then she pulled out a toilet bag covered in green sprigged cotton and gazed at herself critically in the small mirror. The face that stared back at her looked a shade less spruce than usual. Her English rose complexion was still unmarred by two days of fierce Australian sun and her fine, chiselled features and pearly teeth looked much as always, but her hair was damp and bedraggled and her lipstick seemed to have evaporated. Clicking her tongue, Caroline set to work with a comb and some carefully chosen cosmetics to repair the damage. But all the time she was working, a dizzy, bubbling sense of exhilaration was fizzing up inside her like champagne. Two years of hard work and obstinate refusal to quit had brought her to this lonely outback spot, yet it was difficult to believe that it was really happening. Closing her eyes, she let the hot, dust-laden breeze fan her skin. The pungent, aromatic scent of the eucalyptus leaves crept into her nostrils and the shrilling of cicadas rang in her ears. A slow grin crept over her face. Yes, she had definitely left South Kensington far behind. Her eyes fluttered open.

'Caroline Faircroft,' she said aloud, 'this is the biggest adventure you've ever had. And if you only can find that plant, a lot of children may owe their lives to you.'

That thought made her bundle up her toiletries and reach for her lunch pack and map. If she wanted to be at Anapunga by nightfall, she had a lot of hard driving still to do. Frowning, she unfolded the map, took a gulp of lemon mineral water and bit into a chicken sandwich. The sandwich was warm and limp and a cloud of flies immediately buzzed around her face to try and share it, but she was too absorbed in her map-reading to care. It was after two o'clock now and she probably had four hours of daylight left. Four hours at, say, forty miles an hour over these roads. No, she'd never do it. It must be a distance of over two hundred miles. Unless... Her eye fell on the broken black line that marked a four-wheel-drive track. The turn-off couldn't be more than a few miles from here, and it would cut the distance in half. Of course, the ride might be a bit rough, but wasn't that half the fun of it? Biting into a lush slice of pawpaw, she looked more closely at the wavering, broken line.

Rough! she thought an hour later. This isn't rough, it's lunar terrain. I must have been out of my mind to tackle it! Through the dust-smeared windscreen she saw a landscape of red earth, saltbush and shimmering blue sky. Once a kangaroo leapt carelessly over the bonnet of the jeep and several times flocks of sulphur-crested cockatoos rose noisily into the air at her approach. But most of the time she had nothing to occupy her mind but the need to endure the bone-jolting bumps and crashes and to swing the steering-wheel whenever a really huge crater appeared in front of her. She would have turned around and gone back to the highway, except that there was nowhere to turn safely. So she clung grimly to the wheel and continued on, telling herself that it must get better soon. It didn't. It got worse—until shortly after four o'clock, when she breasted a rise and found herself bucketing down a slope strewn with boulders as large as beach balls. Panic flared through her as she looked in vain for a clear track through the debris. For an instant all seemed well, as the rocks toppled beneath the wheels like giant skittles, then suddenly a huge boulder rolled in front of the jeep. Caroline gasped and swung the steering-wheel, but it was too late. There was a loud, grinding crash and her head hit the windscreen.

For ten seconds she sat completely motionless with shock, as a lump the size of an egg leapt into being on her forehead. Then she clenched her fists, opened her mouth and let out a low wail.

'Damn!' she cried, beating her fists on the steering-wheel. 'Damn, damn, damn!'

She climbed out to inspect the damage. Aiming a furious kick at the front tyre of the vehicle, she crouched down on her haunches and peered underneath the jeep. She had taken a course in emergency vehicle main-tenance and knew all about changing tyres and using

tights as a fan-belt. But what she saw now appalled her.
Half the internal parts of the vehicle had been ripped
out and were dangling uselessly against the rock that
had damaged them. Caroline rose to her feet and pressed
the back of her fist against her mouth. She would never
be able to fix it. Never. And, although she had three
days' supplies of food and water in the vehicle, this
seemed like an awfully isolated place. What if nobody
came in three days? Fear descended on her with a cold,
icy touch...

Two hours later Caroline had slipped into an uneasy doze
in the shade of the jeep. Her sleeping-bag and a groundsheet were not enough to soften the rocks beneath her,
but the thought of lying down in the vehicle was unbearable. Beneath the blazing afternoon sun, it had
turned into a furnace like a baker's oven. Licking her
dry lips, Caroline moaned drowsily and groped for the
water canteen. Hauling herself up on one elbow, she tried
to sip sparingly at its now lukewarm contents, but her
thirst was so overpowering that she found herself gulping
greedily. With a determined movement she screwed the
cap back on the bottle.
    Then she shaded her eyes and stared down at the plain
that spread out below her, like an old, threadbare red
carpet. She was hoping for something that would in-
dicate the presence of water—a green patch of vegetation, or a meandering line that might mark a creek
bed. But there was nothing. Only the intense, hurtful
blue of the sky, the shimmering red immensity of the
plain, and, in one insignificant corner far to the east, a
small cloud of red dust as if something were moving.
Moving! Suddenly Caroline sprang into feverish action,
rummaging in the jeep for anything that might attract
attention. She blared the horn furiously, she leapt around
on top of the ridge, waving a red T-shirt, she flashed her
make-up mirror and screamed herself hoarse. Then she
stood with her eyes shaded, trying desperately to focus

on that tiny cloud. It might only be a breeze stirring up the sand or animals changing their feeding ground, but it was impossible to tell. The light was so clear and bright that it dazzled her, and the colours of the land and sky were as lurid as a badly adjusted colour television. With a cry of exasperation, Caroline climbed into the jeep and emerged again with her field binoculars. But what she saw made her lower the binoculars and shake her head in disbelief.

'I must be getting heat-stroke,' she whispered uncertainly. 'That can't really be a man in white robes riding a camel...!'

Yet as she watched in horrified fascination the dust cloud grew larger and larger. Incredulously Caroline scrambled down the slope and stood at the foot of it, gaping at the apparition that came hurtling towards her. The camel's legs seemed to fly out sideways at every stride and the rider's white robes shimmered blindingly against the dazzling backdrop of the desert. As the pair grew closer, the animal slackened speed and the man shouted a hoarse command in some strange language. They slowed to an ungainly jog and then came to a halt. The camel stretched its neck haughtily and gave a long, grumbling cry. There was another sharp command in the unknown tongue and it fell to its knees, then lowered itself into a crouch so that the man could dismount. Caroline's heart beat faster as she watched the tall, lean figure striding across the sand towards her. Who on earth could he be? Some eccentric Arab sheikh, perhaps? And how could she possibly communicate with him if he didn't speak English?

But as he walked towards her he unwound the burnous that protected his face from the choking dust and she saw that he could not possibly be a genuine Arab. His hair was as blond as ripe corn and his eyes were the colour of blue speedwell. But what struck her most about him was the air of controlled rage that seemed to radiate out from him. Perhaps it was that which made Caroline hurry towards him, babbling like a nervous schoolgirl in a high, clear voice.

'Oh, thank goodness! I can't tell you how glad I am to see you...'

Her voice trailed away in the face of his grim, unsmiling silence. With barely hidden disdain, he let his eyes rove down over every detail of her figure from the lump on her forehead to the pearl and gilt earrings in her ears and the smart leather sandals from a boutique in Mayfair.

'You bloody fool!' he said contemptuously.

For a full minute they stood surveying each other. In spite of the stranger's accusation, Caroline was anything but a fool, and his obvious disdain touched her on the raw. Her initial relief at seeing him gave way to a feeling of dismay, but she was adept at hiding her feelings. Smiling hesitantly, she held out her hand.

'How do you do?' she said in a cool, sweet voice with barely a tremor in it. 'My name is Caroline Faircroft. I'm a botanist from London.'

He looked wary, but he took her slim, creamy fingers and crushed them in his huge, calloused hand.

'Adam Fletcher,' he replied curtly. 'I own this land we're standing on.'

I'll bet you do, thought Caroline despairingly. Along with the rest of the continent, judging by your manner. She withdrew her hand from his and surreptitiously massaged her fingers. In spite of the dislike that was beginning to grow in her, she knew perfectly well that Adam Fletcher was her only hope of getting out of this disaster and continuing with her expedition. If anyone could find a mechanic to repair her jeep, he would be the man. Or perhaps he could even fix it himself. She stole a glance at his powerful frame and shrewd, rugged features. He looked capable of just about anything. Caroline cleared her throat.

'I wonder if you could advise me what I should do about the jeep,' she said nervously. 'I'm afraid I've broken something underneath it and I really haven't a hope of fixing it myself. Is there anywhere around here where I could find a mechanic?'

He gave a low, explosive growl of laughter that made her wince. Then, astonishingly, he took her by the shoulders and almost lifted her clean off the ground with the force of his grip.

'You're English, aren't you?' he demanded in an exasperated voice.

'Yes!' she retorted defensively. 'What's wrong with that?'

He released her and paced across the cracked red earth.

'Nothing,' he muttered, running his hand through his sunbleached hair. 'Still, I suppose it does give you some excuse for being such an utter fool. But not much.'

Caroline flinched at the hostility in his voice and bit her lip.

'Why are you so angry with me?' she demanded.

He sighed and motioned her towards him.

'Let me just explain something to you,' he said. 'Take a look down at the plain there. Go on, use your binoculars and get a good, sweeping view all the way from that mountain ridge down in the south, along the horizon to the east and up to the north. What do you see?'

Caroline obeyed. The land leapt into focus in all its fierce, primitive colour and power.

'Rocks,' she said. 'Red dust, saltbush, gum trees. Blue sky.'

'What else?' insisted Adam Fletcher.

'Nothing,' she replied in bewilderment.

'Exactly. Nothing—absolutely nothing. Not a sign of human beings for sixty miles or more. And yet you drive out here on a back road completely on your own, without any survival equipment, knowing damn-all about the land and thinking you can find a nice convenient mechanic to mend your vehicle when it breaks down. Well, that's what I call being an utter fool!'

'Now just a minute!' protested Caroline. 'What do you mean "without survival equipment"? It may interest you to know that I have enough food and water in the four-wheel-drive to last for three days. Not to mention a sleeping-bag and camping gear!'

'Oh, jolly good!' exclaimed Adam Fletcher in a heavy parody of an upper-class Englishman. 'That's super, sweetheart, but it simply isn't enough. Did you report at a police station before you set out to tell them where you were going and when you expected to arrive?'

'No,' admitted Caroline unwillingly.

'Was anybody expecting you at your destination who would start a search when you didn't show up by sundown?'

Reluctantly she shook her head.

'Then you've had a very lucky escape!' he snarled. 'It was pure chance that I happened to be in the area and saw the sun glinting off your windscreen. Otherwise you'd probably have been dead by the end of the week.'

'Dead?' echoed Caroline in a horrified voice. Then she rallied. 'That's nonsense! I was on a public road.'

'A public road that often has no traffic on it for two or three months at a time,' he retorted grimly.

She stared at him open-mouthed. Seizing his advantage, he took her by the shoulders and turned her to face the haunting, sunlit landscape from which he had emerged.

'Now you listen to me,' he ordered. 'You're not in Mayfair now. And don't you dare come into this land, thinking you're going to change it to suit yourself. It's great country, none better, but you're the one who's got to change to suit the place, not the other way round. Do you understand me?'

'Yes,' she replied hoarsely.

His hands seemed to burn through her thin T-shirt and she felt a sudden tremor of emotion pass through her. Just what the emotion was she could not quite tell, but it was compounded of elation and terror. As she stood staring out over that vast, primeval country, she felt suddenly awed and transfigured and infinitely lonely. The feeling made her shiver.

'What is it?' demanded Adam Fletcher, swinging her back to face him.

Her shoulders felt suddenly soft and boneless under his grip. She was afraid she might disgrace herself by burrowing into his arms and closing her eyes against that enormous, terrifying emptiness.

'I—I don't know,' she admitted. 'It just seemed to reach out and take hold of me. And I suddenly realised how huge and empty and silent it is. Somehow it makes me feel incredibly insignificant.'

'It does do that,' he agreed. 'But I think it's good for people to feel insignificant once in a while. And the thing to do is surrender to it. Just let yourself go and feel the heartbeat of the country. It isn't empty at all once you get to know it. It's beautiful and cruel and full of life.'

Caroline stared at him, astonished by the visionary flame in his blue eyes as he looked out over the rugged plain.

'Y-you really love this place, don't you?' she faltered. He gave a small, exasperated snort, as if the question were so ridiculous that it didn't deserve an answer. Then he turned on his heel and strode up the loose scree of stones.

'I suppose I'd better see what kind of mess you've made of the four-wheel-drive,' he said brusquely.

Crouching on his haunches, he peered underneath the vehicle and gave a low whistle of dismay.

'Oh, hell,' he exclaimed in disgust. 'When you decide to wreck something, you don't play at it, do you? Do you realise you've ripped the diff out?'

'The what?' echoed Caroline blankly.

'The differential,' he explained. 'That lump of metal that's hanging down on the rock there. It's completely ruined.'

'Can it be fixed?' she asked anxiously.

Adam Fletcher rubbed his chin thoughtfully.

'Maybe,' he agreed. 'Provided we can get somebody out to look at it before the Wet sets in. Of course, once the rain starts, she'll be stuck for months, but there's no use borrowing trouble. Why don't you get your gear together and we'll get moving?'

'Where to?' demanded Caroline

'My place—Winnamurra Station. The homestead's just up the road from there.'

'I thought you said there were no human beings for sixty miles!' she said tartly.

For the first time Adam smiled broadly. A network of tiny lines crinkled into motion around his eyes and creases of amusement furrowed his cheeks. With his even white teeth and rugged features, he looked surprisingly attractive.

'Around these parts, sixty miles is just up the road!' he retorted. 'Now tell me what you want to take and we'll get going. I want to reach a decent campsite before sunset.'

'But how are we going to get there?' blurted out Caroline in a bewildered voice.

Adam Fletcher jerked his head towards the camel, who was staring haughtily at them from the foot of the slope.

'Jedda will take us,' he replied carelessly. 'Now come on—move. But only bring what's really essential.'

Caroline walked hesitantly over to the jeep and opened the back door. A low mutter of exasperation escaped her. Everything in the vehicle was essential, from the high-powered microscope to the small Coleman stove and camp table, but it was obvious that she couldn't carry all of it on a camel's back. Torn by indecision, she picked up a torch and a water canteen, then set down the torch and rummaged under a groundsheet to find her two suitcases full of clothes.

'Hurry up!' urged Adam. 'I haven't got all day!'

'I am hurrying!' she flared.

He picked up a lightweight pack, emptied the contents ruthlessly on to the floor of the vehicle and held the flap open.

'You can have eight kilos,' he said ruthlessly. 'And if you choose badly, you're the one who'll suffer, not me. Now go!'

Why is he so unpleasant? wondered Caroline miserably, as she burrowed frantically through her clothes. Anyone would think I got stranded here just to annoy him. And he doesn't even have the decency to look away while I'm packing my underwear! An incredulous smile flickered across Adam Fletcher's face as he watched a lacy blue wisp of a bra and matching briefs disappear into the pack, followed by the flower-sprigged toilet bag.

'Amazing what some people consider survival gear,' he murmured under his breath.

Defiantly Caroline picked up her portable hairdrier and flung that in too. Then she chose a few items that met with a grudging nod of acceptance from Adam. Three clean T-shirts and matching shorts, a pair of sturdy boots, a compass, matches, a space blanket, tinned food and a can-opener. After that she carefully folded her tiny, portable computer in a blue printed dress and packed that down. Then she wedged a document folder full of papers and snapshots in among the clothes and picked up a polished wooden box the size of a loaf of bread.

'What do you think about my microscope?' she asked hopefully.

He groaned.

'You've got to be kidding,' he replied.

'But I'll need it for my work, and it's worth a fortune!' protested Caroline.

'Well, yes, that's a real problem, with all the street crime we get in these parts,' he agreed. 'Pickpocketing kookaburras, gangs of mugging kangaroos, hit-and-run emus. You never know what might happen to it if you leave it in the jeep.'

She threw him a resentful look and put the microscope back in hiding under a pile of clothes.

'I'm ready,' she announced frostily.

He cleared his throat.

'There is the little matter of a sleeping-bag,' he reminded her. 'Unless you're planning on snuggling up to me tonight. Not that I'm complaining, mind, but is that really what you want?'

Caroline's cheeks burned.

Without a word, she scrambled out of the vehicle, stalked across to the patch of shade where she had been resting and picked up her sleeping bag. In a series of tense, angry movements, she folded it in half and rolled it into a bundle, which she thrust into a drawstring bag.

'I'm ready,' she said again through clenched teeth.

'Good—well, come and have your first camel riding lesson,' invited Adam amiably.

Caroline closed the doors of the jeep and followed him down the slope. Although she didn't want to talk to him any more than she could avoid, curiosity overcame her.

'Why do you ride a camel?' she asked. 'Do you secretly think of yourself as Lawrence of Arabia?'

He swung the burnous over his head and wrapped it mysteriously round his face. Then he strode theatrically away from her, humming the theme music from the film in a surprisingly rich baritone voice. Caroline felt oddly moved by the sound of that wild melody heard against such a setting. Then Adam halted abruptly and let the drapery fall to reveal his sardonically smiling mouth.

'Good heavens, no!' he exclaimed. 'I simply find it a practical way to get around this sort of country. Camels were used a lot here in the old days and there were always

Afghan camel drivers on my grandfather's property. All the old drivers are dead and gone now, but I like to keep up some of the old traditions. Besides, the white robes keep off the sun and the dust. Now let's get you aboard the old girl. Jedda, this is Caroline.'

Caroline recoiled as the camel turned its neck and gave her a long, haughty stare. But Adam's hard brown hands were pressed into her back, so she allowed herself to be hoisted up on to the leather saddle and sat nervously waiting, while he stowed her possessions in the saddlebags. Then he swung his leg casually over the camel's back and put one hard brown arm around Caroline's waist.

'Sorry if I'm crowding you,' he said impersonally. 'This saddle is really only made for one.'

An astonishing medley of sensations shot through Caroline's body as she felt his hold tighten around her. Her throat felt so constricted that she could scarcely breathe and she was intensely aware of the powerful, muscular frame of the man who held her. He smelled of sweat and dust, as she expected, but also of a clean, French tang that suggested a subtle and expensive cologne. Certainly not aftershave. His chin brushed her shoulder as he leaned forward to adjust the bridle and it was like being pricked by a scrubbing-brush. And yet, strangely, the sensation sent an odd thrill through Caroline's body. He was actually quite an attractive man, she thought. In fact most women would probably have found him disturbingly good-looking. But, ever since the break-up of her marriage to Jeremy Hetherington, Caroline had been off men, full stop. Pursing her lips, she sat up very straight and tried to draw away from Adam's hold.

Unfortunately at that moment he uttered some strange command in a foreign language and the camel shot to its feet. Its back feet. The front legs remained neatly folded on the ground and Caroline nearly went sailing

over its head. Naturally Adam caught her and hauled
her humiliatingly back into place.

'If you can't ride, surely to heaven you can have
enough brains to hold on!' he snapped.

'I *can* ride!' she retorted furiously. 'I just didn't learn
on an animal that's a hundred and twenty hands high
with legs like a collapsible card table.'

'Well, try learning now!' he ordered.

And, after another strange command, the camel was
up on both sets of legs and suddenly sprinting towards
the horizon. It was a surprisingly exhilarating sensation,
although Caroline felt certain she was going to shoot off
into orbit at any moment. Saltbush and rocks flashed
past, and once a frill-necked lizard went racing energetically beside them like a cocky small boy, offering a
challenge. But after a while Adam pulled on the reins
and the camel slackened speed.

'I don't want to wear her out,' he explained, his voice
slightly muffled by the burnous that was wrapped around
his face. 'See that ridge up there? If we can cross that
by nightfall, I'll be happy. There's good water on the
other side and a place where we can camp. It's called
Walter's Springs.'

As the camel lurched steadily on towards the ridge,
Caroline began to understand how apt the name 'ship
of the desert' really was. The swaying motion was making
her feel decidedly queasy, and the burning radiance of
the sun didn't help. Although she was wearing a wide-
brimmed hat and sunscreen, her clean T-shirt was already
plastered to her body with sweat and her eyes were aching
from the glare. Sighing fretfully, she drew an embroidered handkerchief out of her shorts pocket and
dabbed at her face and neck.

'Your skin's going to be scorched by tomorrow
morning,' said Adam. 'Here, you'd better take this!'

In a series of fluid movements, he stripped the white
robe from his body without even dismounting and
wrapped it round her shoulders. She gave a startled gasp

and almost fell off the camel, wondering if his spon-
taneous gift had left him totally naked. But twisting
around, she saw that he was still dressed. Not in the sort
of embroidered caftan that she somehow expected, but
in ragged Levi shorts, an army shirt and sturdy boots.

'What about you?' she demanded.

'My skin is pretty tanned,' he said. 'I think it can
survive for an hour or so. But the last thing I want is
for you to get a bad case of sunburn or heat-stroke.'

Caroline felt surprisingly moved by his brusque
concern. She was just clearing her throat to murmur
some appropriate reply when he ruined everything.

'You're enough trouble as it is,' he finished scathingly.

She fumed silently as they picked their way up the
ridge, but she had to concentrate so hard to avoid
slipping off the camel that she had little time to worry
about how much she disliked Adam Fletcher. And when
they were halfway down the other side, she saw something which drove all thoughts of their feud out of her
mind. Suddenly, in a blaze of pink and orange glory,
the sunset arrived. Incredible puffballs of cloud chased
each other across the skies like gold and scarlet sheep
and the colours overhead ranged from forget-me-not-
blue to wild rose.

'Oh, can't we stop and look at it?' she begged.

'No, we cannot!' Adam retorted. 'I want to get down
out of these rocks before Jedda breaks a leg. *Yiha!* Come
on, sweetie!'

Before long they descended from the ridge on to level
ground, and to Caroline's relief she heard the sound of
running water. As they skirted the next outcrop of rock,
they came upon an inviting green pool set like a gem-
stone in the arid landscape. Here the golden rocks gave
way to lush green ferns and water cascaded in a glittering arc from a rugged crag into the pool below. Ripples
of sunlight danced up the rock walls.

'Oh, it's lovely!' breathed Caroline. 'Can we swim?'

'Sure,' agreed Adam, bringing the camel to a halt with a tug on the bridle. 'Down, Jedda! Of course we'll have to watch out for crocodiles.'

'Crocodiles?' she echoed in a horrified voice. She had been on the point of alighting from the kneeling beast, but now she drew her legs hastily up on to the saddle.

'Don't panic,' urged Adam wearily. 'We keep them down pretty efficiently round here, but you can never afford to get complacent. Still, you probably have no more chance of getting eaten by a croc tonight than you have of getting run over by a London bus on your way to work. So there's no point getting scared, is there?'

'No, I suppose not,' she agreed uneasily.

Except that London buses don't have large, vicious teeth and tiny reptilian eyes and horrible scaly tails, she thought in dismay. And there are traffic lights and underpasses in London where people can cross the road safely.

'Well, don't just sit there!' urged Adam. 'Strip off and have your swim before it gets dark.'

He hauled her unceremoniously off the camel's back, groped in one of the saddlebags and thrust her lightweight pack at her. Caroline stared down at it with a stricken expression.

'I don't think I will swim, thank you,' she gabbled in a high, frightened voice. 'You go ahead. I'll—I'll light the campfire or something.'

His face twisted into a sardonic grin.

'You'd probably do that about as well as you drive a jeep,' he said sceptically. 'I'll tell you what—if you're really worried about crocs, I'll stand guard for you. How about that?'

And he drew a long, dangerous-looking rifle out of a leather holster strapped to Jedda's side.

'But I've forgotten my swimsuit!' bleated Caroline.

'Oh come on!' he exclaimed. 'Do you seriously think it's going to turn me on to see your irresistible body flashing by naked, underwater, in fading light, at a distance of twenty metres? Now have you finished your little song-and-dance routine, or would you like to perform a bit longer while this poor camel sits here waiting for a drink?'

Scarlet with mortification, Caroline flounced across to the pool with her bag. She didn't dare go into the thicket of trees to undress in case there were crocodiles lurking, but she turned her back on Adam. Her fingers shook as she peeled off her T-shirt. Damn the man! Damn him, damn him, damn him! Why did he have to be so rude and hateful? Turn him on, indeed! For one furious moment she was tempted to strip completely naked and saunter past him on her way to the pool just to show him how little she cared. But some remaining vestige of caution held her back. After all, she really didn't know him, and anything might happen. But a swift glance down at her underwear reassured her. Really, she was perfectly decent. Her pink butterfly-printed briefs and matching bra were no more revealing than any bikini. With a defiant toss of her head, she ran down into the water.

After the first shock, it was deliciously cool and re-freshing. She dived and spun round, enjoying the silken caress of the water as it sluiced the dust from her hot, sticky skin. When she felt thoroughly clean again, she stood up and stretched luxuriously while she squeezed the water out of her hair. In spite of her resolve not to look at Adam, her eyes strayed downstream to the spot where he was standing with the camel. He raised the rifle in ironic salute, and the gesture sent a sudden jolt of fear through her body. She glanced hastily around, but could not see any crocodiles. Ducking her head under-water, she swam to the bank and hauled herself out.

To her dismay, she found that he was standing by her scattered pile of clothes with one hand on his belt buckle.

'My turn now,' he said with a mocking smile. 'Now mind you don't get too turned on, Miss Faircroft, be-cause it so happens that I've forgotten my swimsuit too!'

Caroline gasped at this insolence, but before she could even turn away he had stripped off his Levi shorts and flung them on the ground. Unfortunately he didn't have the decency to stop there, but immediately followed suit with his underwear. Caroline caught a brief, horrified glimpse of a magnificent male body, then he strode brazenly over the ground and plunged into the water. As she snatched up her towel and buried her face in its sunwarmed folds, she could not help glancing at the figure churning across the pool in a fast, stylish Australian crawl. Reaching the waterfall at the end, Adam rose to his feet and stood rotating luxuriously under its gleaming cascade. Even from a distance of twenty metres Caroline could see the athletic perfection of his body, lit by the red glow from the setting sun. The muscles in his arms and back stood out like steel cables and his powerful chest led down to a trim waist and narrow hips. The rest of his body vanished out of sight below the water, which was probably just as well, since Caroline was suddenly hit by a totally uncharacteristic fantasy. For one insane moment she wondered what it would be like if Adam kissed her. A thrill of desire shot through her as she imagined the pressure of that rock-hard chest and those muscular golden arms. She did not even realise that she was staring blatantly at him until his voice rang out over the water.

'Keeping an eye out for crocs, are you? That's the spirit!'

Overwhelmed by embarrassment, Caroline hurried to dry and dress. By now the sun was on the point of vanishing over the ridgetop and the air was cooling noticeably. She was suddenly aware of an uncomfortable array of sensations—hunger, thirst, the insistent throbbing of her bruised forehead and a weak, rubbery feeling in her legs from the camel ride. Unable to cope with setting up a proper camp, much less confronting Adam Fletcher again, she unrolled her groundsheet and lay down. Just five minutes' rest, she thought, then I'll deal with that outrageous man. Just five minutes...

She woke to a fragrance so savoury that it made her mouth water. Yawning, she sat up and pushed her hair out of her eyes, and discovered that Adam was waving a white enamel plate full of stew under her nose.

'I thought that'd bring you round,' he said with satisfaction. 'I was going to let you just sleep, but I think you need something inside you. Here, take the plate and I'll get you a piece of damper to go with it.'

'What is it?' asked Caroline eagerly, pushing some chunks of white meat around and inhaling their delicious aroma. 'It smells super!'

'It's goanna,' replied Adam.

She recoiled.

'Goanna? You mean those huge scaly lizards that run around on the rocks?'

'Yes. And don't turn up your nose until you've tried it.'

Doubtfully Caroline screwed up her courage and took a small mouthful of the stew. But the first taste dispelled her doubts.

'It is good!' she agreed in surprise. 'Rather like chicken, actually.'

'Yes. It beats freeze-dried chilli con carne any day, if you ask me,' said Adam. 'Here, have a bit of damper with it.'

He dug something that looked like a large grey stone out of the coals at the centre of the fire, but when the ashes were brushed off it proved to be some kind of golden-brown loaf. Breaking it apart, he handed Caroline a large wedge.

'Ooh!' she squealed. 'That's hot!'

It was hot. Hot and delicious, crusty on the outside and warm and moist within. As she chewed and swallowed, Caroline felt a profound sense of well-being and contentment creeping through her. The campfire crackled cheerfully, sending up showers of red-gold sparks, and high overhead the velvety blue sky blazed with white stars. Closing her eyes for a moment, she heard the rhythmic splash of the waterfall and the stealthy rustle of some night-time animal prowling through the bushes. A faint tremor of doubt attacked her.

'You don't think that's a crocodile, do you?' she asked nervously.

'No,' retorted Adam firmly. 'Now have a cup of tea and stop panicking.'

With a forked stick he lifted the blackened tin billy off the fire and poured the boiling water carefully into an enamel mug with a tea-bag in it.

'There you go,' he said. 'You can have a few jelly beans with it if you like. They'll give you energy.'

'Thanks,' said Caroline.

She ate the rest of her odd meal in silence, dreamily watching the way Adam's shadow loomed up against the silver trunk of a eucalyptus tree whenever he moved to throw more wood on the fire. In the glowing orange light, she surveyed him thoughtfully from under her lashes. He must be about thirty-four or thirty-five, she decided, but it provoked her to think that she knew so little about him. Was he married, for instance? Did he have children? Somehow those ideas both sent a tremor of disquiet through her. Of course, she could have asked him, but some innate shyness held her back. And besides, she was almost dropping with fatigue. A sudden yawn caught her unawares and she blinked and stretched. Glancing up, she saw that Adam was watching her with an unreadable expression on his face.

'You look worn out,' he said curtly. 'You'd better turn in.'

'But I was going to wash the dishes,' she protested.

'That's not a lot of use to me,' he pointed out brutally. 'And you're going to be a complete drag on me tomorrow unless you get some rest tonight. So just stop bleating and go to sleep. OK?'

'Just as you like,' retorted Caroline in a freezing tone.

Burrowing down into her sleeping-bag, she turned her back pointedly on him. For a few minutes there, when he was offering her food and making her tea, he had seemed quite human, even nice. But obviously it was like feeding and watering the camel. He didn't do it because he enjoyed her company but simply because he couldn't afford to have her break down out in the desert. He's unfeeling! thought Caroline angrily—totally and completely unfeeling! Well, the sooner we get back to his homestead, the sooner I can hire another jeep and continue with my expedition and I'll never have to see Mr Smart Alec Fletcher again. Which suits me perfectly! And if only I can find that plant, everything will go splendidly...

The thought of the plant kept her awake for a long time, so that the crescent moon had travelled far across the sky before she slipped into a light doze. Long afterwards she opened her eyes and saw the ghostly moonlight reflected off the eucalyptus tree and the silent waters of the pool. Her hip was aching from contact with the hard ground and she was just beginning to turn over when something caught her eye in the shadows at the edge of the bank. Something that made her blood freeze in her veins. A long, motionless shape that might have been a log, except for the tiny, dark orb of an eye that just cleared the surface of the water. For a long, long moment Caroline lay paralysed by terror, unable even to move. Then in a sudden, ferocious lunge, the crocodile surged out of the water and came hurtling towards her, its jaws wide and snapping. With a bloodcurdling scream, she leapt to her feet and frantically tore her way free of the heavy sleeping-bag.

'For heaven's sake! What is it?' demanded Adam.

'A crocodile! A crocodile! Look, there!'

She was still struggling with the sleeping-bag when his arms came round her and pulled her back to the ground. He gave her a small, impatient shake.

'There's no crocodile, Caroline. You've been dreaming!' he said in an exasperated voice.

'But I saw it!'

'No, you didn't. You dreamt it. Look, see for yourself.'

Shuddering back into wakefulness, she scanned the moonlit water suspiciously. But it was as calm and smooth as a bowl of milk. Not a crocodile in sight. A tremor of relief went through her body.

'I-I'm sorry,' she muttered hoarsely. 'I could have sworn...'

'Never mind,' said Adam. 'It's all over now. So you can stop shaking.'

She became aware that his powerful hands were gripping her shoulders and another involuntary tremor ran through her. With a low growl of laughter, he drew her against him and stroked her hair. His touch was surprisingly comforting, and she gave an uneven sigh and let herself go limp against him. Cradling her soothingly in his arms, he kissed her gently on the cheek.

At least, it began gently. But what followed took them both by surprise. Still half asleep and dimly aware that Adam had saved her from the terror of the crocodile, Caroline turned her mouth to his. Her lips met his urgently and her mouth opened. She heard his swift, surprised intake of breath, then he dragged her against him and kissed her as she had never been kissed in her life. The muscles in his arms were like steel cables and she was conscious of a raw, blazing sexuality that he was barely able to control. With a sudden thrust, he took possession of her mouth, and then his questing lips moved down the slender column of her throat. Caroline shuddered with excitement and pressed herself instinctively against him. A soft whimper escaped her and her eyelids fluttered shut as his lips continued their wanton, teasing exploration.

In that moment her whole body caught fire and she welcomed him to her with eager, tremulous kisses. Adam made a muffled sound deep in his throat and dragged her fiercely against him. But as his mouth moved down on to hers and the dark outline of his head blotted out the stars, a surge of panic overtook her. Vivid memories swept over her of those last dreadful weeks with Jeremy, and she was suddenly trapped in a net of disgust and horror. Struggling violently, she pushed Adam away.

'No, don't, don't!' she cried. 'I can't! You don't understand! I can't go through with it!'

He stared down at her incredulously, his face a contorted mask of desire and disbelief. His arms moved forward to hold her, but she struck them away.

'Let me go!' she begged. 'Please, please let me go!'

His eyes raked her body and for a moment she thought he would go ahead anyway—and almost longed for it, welcomed it as a chance to lay her fears to rest. Then he rose slowly to his feet and let out his breath in a hoarse, uneven sigh.

'I don't understand you,' he said bitterly.

And turned away.

CHAPTER TWO

NEXT morning Caroline woke with a vague feeling of uneasiness. At first she could not remember what was upsetting her, then the events of the previous night came back in an embarrassing rush. Climbing out of her sleeping-bag, she padded across the clearing to the spot where Adam was crouching by the fire, frying pancakes.

'Look, about last night,' she faltered. 'I'm awfully sorry. I really didn't——'

'Don't think about it,' he cut in. 'I don't intend to.'

And he turned his back on her and went on deliberately tending his breakfast. It was a response which was to set the pattern for all their encounters during the next two days. Adam obviously did not want to hear Caroline's explanations, and since he could not simply go off and abandon her, he did the next best thing. He withdrew behind a wall of indifferent silence and spoke to her only when it was strictly necessary.

Consequently she felt an overwhelming sense of relief when they reached the homestead at Winnamurra late in the afternoon nearly two days later. Her first clue that they were near the homestead did not come from any statement by Adam. Instead she saw the sunlight coruscating off the tin roof of a weatherboard house set among weeping peppercorn trees. As they came up the red dust track which led to the homestead, a couple of dogs in wooden kennels began a loud chorus of barking. In a moment everybody seemed to be conscious of their arrival and a group of Aboriginal children were hanging over a large gate, waving and giggling shyly. Moments later a black man dressed in Levi jeans, a checked shirt and a wide-brimmed hat came strolling out of a barn. He smiled a welcome.

'G'day, Adam. Who's this that you picked up out on the range, eh?'

'G'day, Danny,' replied Adam curtly, sliding off the camel's back and gesturing at Caroline with his thumb. 'This is Caroline Faircroft. Her four-wheel-drive broke down on the Anapunga track. She'll only be staying a day or two until I can get her sent off to Darwin. Caroline, this is Danny Japulula, my head stockman.'

Caroline felt a quick flare of dismay at Adam's assumption that she could be posted off to Darwin like a parcel, but this didn't seem the right time to make a fuss about it.

'How do you do?' she said, reaching down from the camel's back to shake hands.

'Nice meeting you, missus,' murmured Danny. 'You was real lucky the boss found you. She's pretty crook country out there, if you don't know how to look after yourself. And how's me old girl Jedda, eh?'

'Jedda's fine,' replied Adam swiftly. 'Give her a feed and then let her out in the paddock, will you, Danny? I'll talk with you about the stock out by Grainger's Ridge as soon as I've got a minute, but there's a few problems I have to sort out first. I need to order a cattle truck to take those two-year-old heifers across to Alan Webb's property. And I've got to phone up about some more tick dip for the steers we've been running at Walter's Springs. And then there's this business of Caroline to fix up. But I suppose I'll be free in an hour or so, if you can spare me some time then.'

'No worries,' said Danny, stretching out his hand to take the camel's bridle. 'Down, Jedda!'

'Come on, Caroline,' ordered Adam. 'I want to get your travel arrangements worked out.'

I'll bet you do, thought Caroline dejectedly. Just as soon as you can spare a bit of time from the far more fascinating subjects of cattle trucks and tick dip. Well, I'm not going to give up quite so easily as that! Her

mouth tightened and she flung up her head with uncon-
scious grace. Adam scowled at the sight.

'Give me your hand!' he rapped out as the camel knelt.

Even that brief, hostile touch sent a searing current
of warmth through Caroline's entire body, but there was
definitely nothing flirtatious in Adam's manner. The
moment he was sure she was safely on her feet, he
dropped her hand like a live coal, unfastened the saddlebags and strode towards the house with one over each
shoulder. Caroline almost had to run to keep up with
him.

Just what she had expected from an outback homestead she wasn't really sure, but the house was surprisingly welcoming in a rather spartan way. It was built on
wooden stilts to allow the air to circulate and the wet
season rains to wash harmlessly away, so she had to
follow Adam up a wide set of stairs leading to a veranda
with a panoramic view over the landscape. Swooping
eaves sheltered the house from the fierce heat, and there
was a scattering of cane chairs and loungers set in the
shade. The front door led straight into a huge open-plan
sitting-room furnished with deep leather couches and
cowhide rugs scattered on a polished wooden floor. At
the far end of the room was a dining area which also
overlooked the veranda. But Adam gave her little time
to look around. Hustling her past an archway which revealed a well equipped kitchen, he ushered her into the
central hall. Brass and rattan ceiling fans swished
overhead, and the atmosphere was pleasantly cool and
dim. Adam dropped the saddlebags amid an untidy
clutter of leather boots, stockwhips, hardware catalogues and cowboy hats that lay on an old settee in an
alcove. Then he rummaged in a pine linen cupboard built
into the wall nearby and produced a couple of thick
towels, which he tossed to Caroline.

'Come and I'll show you your bedroom,' he muttered, retrieving her pack from the saddlebag and slinging
it over his shoulder.

He strode off down the hall again, and once more she had to hurry to keep up. As he walked, he spoke in the mechanical monotone of a tour guide.

'Storeroom, office, main bathroom, spare bedroom, my bedroom. And this one is yours.'

Throwing open a door, he stood aside for her to enter the room.

'There's another bathroom through there,' he said, indicating a door at the far end of the room. 'I usually eat about eight o'clock, so just come out when you're ready. If you need me before that, I'll be either in the stockyard behind the house or in my office. Now, is there anything else you want?'

'No, thank you,' said Caroline in a subdued voice.

He was obviously anxious to get away from her and, absurdly, that touched her on the raw. As he edged out the door, a pulse was beating violently at his right temple and his face wore a grim, strained expression. Her resentment towards him suddenly melted as she realised how ridiculous it was for them to be carrying on this cold war. Impulsively she laid one slender white hand on his muscular arm.

'Adam?' she asked huskily.

'What is it?'

His voice was wary, hostile, giving nothing away.

'I'm sorry about kissing you at the pool the other night,' she said in a rush, 'and then stopping like that. I didn't mean it to happen.'

'I know you didn't,' retorted Adam in a hard voice. 'But don't worry, Caroline. I may have misunderstood your signals once, but I don't intend to look a fool twice in a row.'

He turned as if to go, but her slim fingers restrained him.

'Wait!' she begged. 'Look, Adam, this is silly. We can't keep hating each other in a place like this where we're thrown together all the time. It's too ridiculous for words. And besides, I feel as if it's awfully ungracious

of me to fight with you. After all, you did save my life,
and you've really been very kind to me.'

His forehead creased into a frown and his blue eyes
narrowed sceptically.

'Kind!' he sneered, drawing his arm out of her grip
as if he had been stung. 'You've made me feel a lot of
things in the last two days, Caroline. Kind is not one of
them.'

'But can't we be friends?' she asked in an unsteady
voice.

A feral smile drew back the corners of Adam's mouth.

'I don't want to be your friend, Caroline,' he replied
throatily. 'You know damned well what I want from you.'

Suddenly his lean brown hand reached forward and
touched her. Slowly and sensually, he drew his fingers
in a caressing trail down her throat. At his touch, fire
seemed to race through her veins and she was conscious
of an aching warmth uncoiling deep inside her. It was
all she could do not to move sensually into his arms.

'Don't,' she breathed in a suffocating voice.

He smiled bleakly.

'No, it's just not on, is it?' he challenged. 'And if you
think I can be your friend with that kind of a current
between us, you're even more of a fool than I suspected.
No, sweetheart, the best I can offer you is a temporary
suspension of hostilities until you get the hell out of here.
And frankly, the sooner that happens, the better!'

The door slammed violently behind him, and Caroline
winced. Left alone, she collapsed wearily on the bed and
looked around her. Talking to Adam Fletcher was rather
like banging one's head against a brick wall—unpro-
ductive, painful and totally undignified. From the first
moment she met him it had been obvious that he regarded her as a nuisance and resented her presence on
his land. Yet in spite of that, he had actually taken very
good care of her.

Images flashed into her mind of Adam offhandedly draping his white robes around her to protect her from sunburn, Adam waking her to offer a plate of fragrant stew, Adam stroking her hair and soothing her when she jumped up screaming in the grip of a nightmare. But that last picture made her cringe, for another one followed hot on its track. She saw herself lifting her mouth to Adam's kiss and clinging urgently to him. The memory made her groan aloud. How could I have done it? she thought, appalled. If only I hadn't been half asleep and scared out of my wits, I wouldn't have been so rash. And yet there was some animal magnetism about Adam Fletcher, some surly masculine aura that must make women lose their heads all the time. Caroline went hot and cold at the thought of how close she had come to surrendering to him. If you could call it surrender, when she was the one who had started it all. And with a man she hardly knew! For heaven's sake, she hadn't even slept with Jeremy until they had been engaged for nearly a year. And in the three years since her divorce, there had been nobody. Nobody! So why on earth should she suddenly start melting like snow in the desert under Adam Fletcher's touch?

After all, she definitely wasn't interested in a casual affair. Or even in a serious affair, for that matter. If she had come out of the fiasco of her marriage with one thing clear in her mind, it was that she had suffered enough. Love, sex, marriage, men were all things other women could tie themselves in knots about if they wanted to. Not Caroline Faircroft. She was a career woman, first, last and always. And she should have made that clear to Adam Fletcher instead of flinging herself at him. It wasn't even as though they had anything in common. The whole episode was just a dreadful mistake.

'I wish I hadn't done it,' she muttered, slamming her fist into the palm of her other hand.

And it wasn't only embarrassment that bothered her. Of course, it was bad enough to know she must soon go out and smile and talk to Adam with the memory searing through her of how he had crushed her against him. But even worse was the problem of dealing with his antagonism. Caroline was shrewd enough to know she had ruined all hope of friendship between them. Adam had obviously been seething for the past two days, but the depth of his bitterness surprised her. Even if he had interpreted her rejection as a personal insult, it was hard to see why his hostility should be quite so intense.

Yet this was the man whose grudging hospitality she would have to accept at least until she could hire another vehicle. Not only that. Adam had been making ominous noises about arranging for her to travel back to Darwin. If he organised a ride for her, how could she possibly insist that she wanted to stay on at Winnamurra? And yet where else could she go? Most of her camping equipment was still out in the wrecked jeep, and she had some idea now of how harsh this country could be. No, if her expedition was to have any chance of success, she simply must win Adam Fletcher's support. And that meant somehow defusing the antagonism between them—a depressing prospect. Yet experience had taught her how useless it was to wallow in depression, so Caroline mentally shook herself and turned her attention to something else: the room she was sitting in.

It could have been quite a pleasant place, except that it was totally featureless. The walls were painted a neutral shade of cream without a single picture or hanging to relieve their blankness. Beige curtains were drawn back from floor-to-ceiling windows which opened on to a wooden deck, shaded by an overhanging veranda. Built-in cupboards covered one wall, and the only other furniture was the bed and a simple wooden bedside table with a clock radio and reading lamp. Yet the bed was well sprung and clearly expensive, and the sliding doors on the cupboards moved smoothly at the slightest touch. The only hint of individuality in the room was a flower-patterned wallpaper border which ran halfway round the outside of the door-frame and then stopped abruptly. It was as if somebody had started work and become discouraged. To Caroline, who had a natural flair for decorating, the room cried out for the little homely touches that meant so much. Cushions, plants, mirrors, paintings, pretty lampshades, splashes of colour that would give it the stamp of an owner.

Pushing open the bathroom door, she looked around her and sighed. It was exactly what she expected—functional, even luxurious, but totally devoid of character. And the pine windowsill and laminex vanity top were both covered in a fine layer of red dust.

'Oh, what does it matter?' she demanded, glaring at her reflection in the mirrored cabinet above the washbasin. 'What business is it of yours if Adam Fletcher lets his house get dusty? You'll only be here for a couple of days at the most!'

And yet her face wore the brooding, wary expression that she had come to know so well in the months after Jeremy had left her. There was no doubt that Adam's kisses had brought back a flood of bitter memories that she would much rather not confront. Angrily reaching inside the shower, she turned on the taps and was rewarded by a thunderous downpour of warm water. With a little wriggle of anticipation, she tore off her clothes and stepped under the shower. It was marvellous to feel clean again, marvellous to soap every inch of her body and shampoo her hair. After five glorious minutes she climbed out, wrapped herself in the thick fawn bath towel that Adam had given her and padded quietly into the bedroom.

Delving in her pack, she drew out her hairdrier and the folder of photos and documents. As she unwound the cord of the drier, she spread the contents of the folder out on the bed and frowned down at them. If Terry Connor, the art curator at her museum, was right, the plant she was looking for should be found somewhere within a hundred-mile radius of the Winnamurra home-

stead. But that still left an awful lot of ground to cover.
Obviously her only chance of success lay in finding a
new jeep and a local guide to help her—and she had an
uneasy feeling that only Adam Fletcher could arrange
that for her. Well, she hadn't come all this way just to
give up now. Her wide, generous mouth set in a stubborn
line and she pulled the brush determinedly through her
tangled brown hair. Whatever it cost her, she would
simply have to bottle up her antagonism towards Adam
Fletcher and be very, very polite to him tonight.

It was just after eight o'clock when Caroline emerged
into the living-room. As always when she was feeling
insecure, she had taken even more care than usual with
her grooming. Her brown hair flew in buoyant waves
around her face, her grey eyes were highlighted with a
touch of smoky eyeshadow and her full, generous mouth
was glossy with coral lipstick. She wore clip-on gold earrings and a matching pearl and crystal necklace with gold
inserts. There had been little choice as far as her clothes
were concerned, but her one and only dress clung re-
vealingly to her tall, slim figure and its floral print in
tones of deep blue and rust lent colour to her creamy
skin. As she opened the door of the room, she knew she
looked her best, but her insides were still tensing horribly at the prospect of confronting Adam. So it came
as almost an anticlimax to discover that he wasn't there.
Caroline looked around her with a puzzled expression.
The delicious aroma of barbecued steak was wafting into
the room from somewhere, but a cursory glance showed
her that the kitchen and dining alcove were both deserted. Then she heard a sharp whistle from below.

'Come on down if you want to eat,' called Adam's
deep voice from somewhere outside. 'And bring the
salad, will you? I've left it in the fridge.'

Intrigued, Caroline fossicked in the refrigerator and
found a large bowl of delicious-looking salad. Picking
it up, she walked out on to the deck.

'Where are you?' she called.

'Straight downstairs and turn left. And then left again.'

She followed Adam's directions—and let out a low exclamation of delight as she found herself in a paved courtyard next to a gleaming jade swimming-pool. The whole area was lit by concealed white lights and a bed of luxuriant ferns cast dramatic shadows on the paving as she walked across to join Adam. He was standing by a brick barbecue with his back to her, efficiently turning some sizzling meat on a grill. At the sound of her footsteps, he turned around, and her heart gave a sudden lurch. It was the first time she had seen him shaved and dressed in clean clothes, and she wanted to cry out at the unfairness of it. For now he was not just vibrantly masculine with an aura of wild strength about him. He was quite simply irresistible. His thick blond hair was brushed carelessly back from his forehead, revealing features that were both strong and yet perfectly sculpted. In spite of his fairness, he had very dark eyebrows and dark lashes that showed up the startling intensity of his blue eyes. His nose was straight and classic in shape and the corners of his mouth had a mocking twist that was oddly disturbing. Coupled with the animal grace of his lean, muscular body, it was enough to make any woman's heart beat faster. What was worse, he gave her a swift, smouldering glance that left her with the uneasy feeling that she was standing on the edge of a volcano waiting for an eruption. Then his shoulders hunched and he turned away.

'Can I get you a drink?' he asked abruptly. 'I'm having Scotch, but there's gin and tonic or sherry or Campari and soda.'

'Campari and soda, please,' said Caroline, breathing more easily.

Perhaps they could have a pleasant, civilised evening after all without any more emotional collisions, she thought hopefully. And when Adam passed her the glass of Campari, she found herself beginning to relax. The bittersweet flavour of the drink was reassuring. It seemed to take her back to the sort of world she was used to, the world of drawing-rooms and cocktail parties and superficial chatter. Not the strange, harsh, frighteningly intimate world of the outback which she had shared with Adam for the last two days. And yet it seemed totally incongruous to be standing here in a stylish dress sipping a drink from a crystal tumbler amid quite elegant surroundings. It gave her a feeling of unreality as if the pool and the soft, piped music and the luxuriant ferns might suddenly vanish, leaving her alone in the desert with Adam. She glanced surreptitiously around her, giving her head a slight shake.

'What is it?' asked Adam. 'You look stunned.'

She gestured with her glass.

'I can't believe it's all real,' she explained. 'It's such a contrast to the world outside. Like walking into a film set or something.'

He laughed.

'Well, the Territory's a great place to live,' he said. 'But it can be a bit uncomfortable, and I like comfort. So I fixed this place up to suit me. When I'm out on the range, I live rough, but the minute I get home I relax and enjoy myself. The house is a bit of a mess, but I always keep the swimming-pool clean. I've got my priorities right.'

Caroline walked over to the edge of the pool and sat down on the tiled parapet. Then she trailed her fingers in the cool jade green water.

'It's superb,' she marvelled. 'You've thought of everything—even ice and lemon in the drinks. How on earth do you manage that?'

Adam shrugged.

'It's easy enough,' he replied carelessly. 'I make a buying trip to Darwin two or three times a year and I have a very large freezer. In fact, I have four very large freezers. I can offer you everything you could possibly want to eat, from chicken liver pâté with Cointreau to chocolate Bavarian.'

'I wish you would!' she exclaimed. 'I'm starving!'

'Right. Well, let's eat,' agreed Adam. 'Just give me a minute to finish grilling this steak.'

Soon Caroline was staring down at a vast plate laden with sizzling fillet steak, fried mushrooms, a baked potato in foil with a topping of sour cream and chives and a generous helping of fresh salad.

'Well, you may have four enormous freezers,' she marvelled, 'but I still can't believe that you manage to grow lettuce in them.'

Adam shook his head.

'No,' he admitted. 'My neighbour Alan Webb and his wife have a greenhouse. They were here last week and they dropped a few fresh vegetables in. Now, do you fancy a glass of claret with that?'

'Yes, please,' agreed Caroline eagerly.

She watched thoughtfully as Adam poured half an inch of wine into his own glass and swirled it critically under his nose before sipping it. An approving smile spread over his face.

'Yes, I think that's fit to drink,' he said.

Deftly he filled Caroline's glass, leaving space for the wine to breathe.

'Cheers!' he murmured, lifting his glass.

'Cheers,' echoed Caroline, sipping cautiously.

But Adam was right. The wine was not merely fit to drink, it was superb—a full, soft Hunter Valley red of very high quality. Yet Caroline couldn't help but feel taken aback by the discovery. It seemed so incongruous for a wild outback man like Adam Fletcher to be interested in wines.

'This is actually very good,' she said in a surprised voice.

He smiled mockingly.

'But not what you expected?' he demanded shrewdly. 'Did you think I'd have my feet on the table and offer you a swig of cold beer out of a can?'

'No, of course not,' replied Caroline hastily.

But Adam's sly remark was so close to the truth that she felt her cheeks flushing hotly.

'You want to be careful of stereotypes,' he drawled. 'Don't just assume that because I'm a cowboy I'm also an oaf. Or I might assume that because you're a posh young lady with a plum in her mouth, you're also arrogant and pretentious.'

For an instant Caroline sat transfixed, then she let out a soft, unsteady breath.

'Why do you dislike me so much?' she asked, setting down her fork.

He shrugged.

'Dislike is a strong word,' he replied. 'I have nothing personal against you. But I suppose it would be fair to say that I dislike almost everything you stand for.'

'I see,' she said unsteadily. 'And what exactly do I stand for?'

'Ignorance, foolhardiness, the arrogant assumption that you're somehow doing this country a favour just by setting a foot in it. I've seen your kind before.'

Caroline might be shy and reserved by nature, but she wasn't going to take an outright insult lying down. Her grey eyes sparkled angrily.

'I think you're being thoroughly rude,' she protested. 'My kind, indeed! How can you be so sure what "my kind" is anyway? You know practically nothing about me.'

'I know what I've seen with my own eyes,' retorted Adam. 'That you came into this country ill equipped and with no conception of how to survive here. That's the kind of foolhardy behaviour that leads to disaster. You needn't think you're the first half-witted tourist who's got herself into trouble in the Northern Territory. Far from it. There was a family of foreigners only last year who tried to take a short cut like yours, but they weren't as lucky as you. I was with the search party who found them, a week too late. You know, I'm used to finding dead cattle by the road, but when it's a four-year-old child...'

He left the sentence unfinished.

'Oh, no,' whispered Caroline in horror. 'Oh, how dreadful!'

Adam grimaced.

'Well, the lesson is that you must always treat this country with respect,' he pointed out. 'Quite honestly, you did infuriate me, capering around worrying about your microscope and your best clothes, when you should have been thanking your lucky stars you were still alive. You should also have been making up your mind that you'll never do anything so reckless again.'

'I won't!' vowed Caroline fervently.

'In that case, let me say "Welcome to the Territory!"' conceded Adam, offering her his hand across the table.

Somehow that brief, warm handshake seemed to lighten the atmosphere considerably. With relief, Caroline picked up her fork and began eating.

'You said the people who own the greenhouse were your neighbours. Do they live far away?' she asked, trying to steer the conversation back into more cheerful channels.

'The Webbs? No, not that far. About a hundred and twenty miles down the road,' replied Adam, sitting down and retrieving his napkin which had fallen to the ground.

She clicked her tongue incredulously.

'I just can't believe the distances in Australia!' she exclaimed. 'It absolutely stuns me to think that people who live a hundred and twenty miles away could be regarded as your neighbours.'

He shrugged.

'It's all a matter of what you're used to, I suppose,' he said. 'I grew up here, so it seems natural to me. Just nice and spacious, that's all. Nobody looking over your shoulder all the time, no need to worry about appearances or other people's opinions. You can be pretty much your own boss, and that suits me.'

'Have you lived here all your life, then?' asked Caroline.

'Most of it,' he answered. 'Although I did spend a few years knocking around overseas in my twenties. But I grew up on this property, and my heart's always been here. When my father died two years ago, I had to make a choice. Either sell up or move back home and put down roots.'

'Did you have a job somewhere else?' queried Caroline.

'Yes,' answered Adam indifferently. 'In Canberra. But it wasn't really my scene. Too much paper-pushing.'

'What were you doing?' she asked. 'Clerical work in the public service?'

His lips quirked wryly.

'Something like that,' he agreed. 'Now, would you like some of this French mustard?'

'Mmm,' murmured Caroline appreciatively, 'yes, please. Do tell me, Adam, what about your education? I suppose you went to boarding-school, did you?'

He grinned wickedly.

'Eventually,' he replied. 'Mind you, I didn't take too kindly to the idea at first. The day my father was supposed to be driving me to Darwin to catch the plane, I lit out into the bush. And I didn't come back until I was damned sure that I'd missed the start of term.'

'Into the bush?' she echoed, aghast. 'That wild, dangerous country out there? How old were you?'

'Twelve,' said Adam carelessly.

'On your own?' she demanded.

'Not quite,' he replied. 'Danny Japulula was with me. But he was only eleven.'

'How long were you out there?' asked Caroline.

'Ten days.'

'Ten days! Your parents must have been frantic!'

'They weren't too pleased,' agreed Adam with a wicked glint in his eye. 'My father gave me a hell of a hiding when we finally showed our faces again. And it didn't do me a lot of good, because he drove me all the way to Geelong Grammar in Victoria and delivered me in person. And he deducted the cost of the petrol from my allowance. You see, he never gave up on anything he'd set his heart on. And he'd set his heart on seeing me get a good education.'

Caroline gave a gurgle of laughter.

'And did you?' she demanded.

He shrugged.

'That's a matter of opinion,' he admitted. 'The school did its best for me, but I was a pretty tough nut to crack. I never had much use for books back then. But give me a horse or a rifle or a helicopter and I was happy. I was born and bred to the outback life and I didn't want anything else.'

Caroline shook her head at this glimpse of a world so different from her own.

'And when you ran away into the bush, how on earth did you manage to stay alive?' she marvelled. 'Did you take food with you?'

'No,' said Adam. 'We lived off the land. It wasn't too difficult, really. Danny's a terrific bushman, and of course all of us kids had hung around with the Aborigines from the time we were babies, so I wasn't bad at finding bush food myself.'

'All of you?' she echoed curiously. 'Did you have brothers and sisters, then?'

'One brother, one sister—Bruce and Rosemary. Both younger. Bruce is a lawyer in Darwin now and Rosemary's married to a chap with a station not far from here. It's——'

'Don't tell me, let me guess,' interrupted Caroline. 'About a hundred and fifty miles down the road.'

'You've got it!' agreed Adam with a grin.

'What about your mother?' she asked. 'Is she still alive?'

'Yes. She's retired and living in Darwin, but she travels down to Rosemary's place pretty often to cluck over her grandchildren. She didn't get enough fun spoiling us for twenty-five years, so now she's working on the next generation.'

'That sounds lovely,' said Caroline in a wistful voice.

Something in her tone made Adam pause with his wineglass halfway to his mouth.

'What's the matter?' he asked. 'Didn't your mother spoil you rotten too?'

She made a face.

'No, she most definitely did not,' she replied lightly, trying to make a joke out of it. 'My parents split up when I was only four, and my mother wasn't exactly bursting with maternal feelings. Actually she went off to Greece almost immediately with her latest lover and left me with my grandmother. It wasn't a very satisfactory arrangement. My grandmother is a very tight-lipped sort of woman with two big passions in life. One is collecting Dresden china, the other is keeping a spotless house.'

'What?' said Adam, looking horrified. 'And you were how old? Four?'

'Mmm,' agreed Caroline, with an ironic lift of the eyebrows. 'Not an ideal combination—four-year-olds and delicate china. Anyway, she soon overcame the difficulty by packing me off to boarding-school. And, unlike you, I didn't have enough gumption to run away into the bush and live off goannas. Not that there's much in the way of bush or goannas around Belgravia.'

'How old were you?' asked Adam.

'Seven.'

'You poor little brat!' he exclaimed wrathfully. 'It's criminal the way some parents treat their kids. So didn't you ever see your mother again?'

'Oh, yes,' said Caroline carelessly. 'Whenever she was back in London between lovers, she used to come and visit me. And she gave me a rather splendid twenty-first birthday party. But she wasn't really a mother, if you see what I mean. Just a terribly glamorous stranger.'

Adam scowled.

'So what about your father?' he persisted. 'Didn't he ever take any notice of you?'

She wrinkled her nose.

'I suppose so,' she shrugged. 'He paid my school fees and he usually invited me up for a week at Christmas, if he wasn't going away, and sometimes for a week in the summer. He has a large estate in Yorkshire, but he travels fairly frequently.'

'How bighearted of him!' growled Adam. 'I don't know, maybe my ideas are out of date, but in my opinion people shouldn't have children unless they want to share their lives with them.'

A sudden thought struck him.

'How about you?' he demanded. 'Didn't you ever want to marry and have children?'

Caught off guard, Caroline flinched. All the old feelings of pain and betrayal came rushing back. In fact she had wanted children desperately, but Jeremy had never been keen on the idea, and before she could talk him around, the marriage had been hopelessly on the rocks. Yet she didn't want to reveal all this heartache to a stranger.

'I was married for a while,' she said in a clipped, brittle voice, 'but it didn't work out. There were no children. I suppose it's just as well really, considering how important my career is to me.'

'I see,' replied Adam thoughtfully. 'So that's it, is it? You'd never give it another try?'

Caroline toyed with her glass, staring into the ruby liquid as if it contained shadows of the past. Then with an abrupt movement of her wrist she drained the last half-inch.

'No,' she said defiantly. 'From here on my career is the only thing that matters to me.'

He frowned disapprovingly.

'You shouldn't say that,' he reproved her. 'You're still young and you're damned good-looking. I'll bet there'd be dozens of men falling over themselves to marry you.'

'Perhaps,' retorted Caroline indifferently. 'But, as I said, I've no intention of every marrying again.'

Adam picked up the claret bottle.

'More wine?' he asked.

She shook her head, and he refilled his own glass.

'So tell me about this career that's going to occupy the rest of your life,' he invited with just a touch of mockery. 'You're a botanist, you said?'

'That's right,' agreed Caroline eagerly. 'I read botany at Cambridge and after I took my degree I got a job at the Morrow Museum in Kensington. I've been there six years now. I got my doctorate a couple of years ago.'

'I see,' murmured Adam, sipping his wine. 'So what brought you all this way out to Australia? Did you just fancy an unusual holiday?'

It was the opening she had been waiting for. Setting her knife and fork side by side on her empty plate, she clasped her hands under her chin and leant forward.

'No, it's not a holiday at all,' she explained. 'It's really more in the nature of a scientific excursion. I've come to look for a plant.'

'A plant?' he echoed. 'What kind of plant?'

'Well, it doesn't really have a name yet, because it hasn't been scientifically described,' explained Caroline. 'But it's a herbaceous perennial that's rather similar to a lily.'

'So what does it look like?' he asked.

'Oh, it's got a few basal, grassy leaves and then it rises to a branched scape thirty to eighty centimetres. It has racemose orange flowers about two centimetres across with three delicately crinkled petals, and——'

'Come on!' exclaimed Adam, throwing up his hands in disgust. 'Tell me in plain English.'

'Well, it looks like a small lily with orange flowers and it has a very distinctive caramel-scented perfume,' replied Caroline.

He caught his breath sharply.

'That's a pretty detailed description,' he remarked suspiciously. 'It sounds as if you've already had the plant in your possession.'

'Oh, I have,' she agreed. 'I've studied several specimens of it, but they all died without reproducing. So that's why I'm here to try and find more of them.'

'And why do you want them?' he demanded.

Caroline was so absorbed in marshalling her thoughts that she did not even notice his brusque tone.

'A friend of mine who's a pharmacologist did some clinical trials on the specimens I had, and he was very excited about them,' she answered. 'It's too soon yet to say for sure, but in some ways this plant seems to resemble the Madagascar blue periwinkle, which is used in the treatment of childhood leukaemia. If I can find the plant and it lives up to its promise, it may eventually save thousands of lives.'

Her face was bright, eager, filled with purpose. Adam glanced searchingly at her and then leant back in his chair with a frown on his face.

'Where did you get those specimens you were telling me about?' he challenged.

Caroline gave a rueful laugh.

'Don't ask!' she warned. 'It's all horribly involved. About two years ago an art dealer called Michael Barclay came to the museum where I work with an Aboriginal painting on a sandstone slab which he sold to us. He was an awfully nice chap. Anyway, when the Aboriginal art curator Terry Connor was examining the work, he found some seeds in the cloth it was wrapped in. Terry knew I'd be interested, so he passed them on to me. I managed to grow a batch of plants from them and roped in every scientist I could find to help me study them— including my pharmacologist friend, John Burnett. Of course, we were all wildly excited when his analysis showed the medical potential of the plant, but then problems set in. For some reason the plants just wouldn't set any seeds, so I couldn't raise a second generation of them. And they wouldn't grow from cuttings either. One by one they all died. It was so frustrating! I still can't figure out what went wrong.'

Adam gave a short laugh.

'Maybe if you'd burnt your laboratory to the ground, you'd have worked it out,' he commented.

'What do you mean?' asked Caroline with a puzzled frown.

He rose to his feet and paced across to the barbecue. Then suddenly he seized a pair of tongs, thrust them into the fire and withdrew a red-hot coal.

'There's your answer, Caroline!' he said. 'Fire! The Northern Territory is the thunder and lightning capital of the world. Each year hundreds of lightning strikes set off fires that rage for miles during August and September. All the plants that live here have had to adapt to that in one way or another, and many of them actually benefit from it. Some of them need scorching to open their seed capsules, but your little fire lily actually relies on heat to trigger its seed production.'

Caroline stared at the smoking coal with an astonished expression as Adam dropped it back into the barbecue.

'Of course!' she marvelled. 'How simple. But, Adam, you sound as if you know the very plant I'm looking for. Do you?'

He hesitated for a moment, but her grey eyes were fixed unwaveringly on his.

'Yes,' he admitted unwillingly.

She jumped up from her seat and whooped with joy.

'Adam, that's super!' she cried. 'Can you take me to the place where it grows? I'll pay you for it!'

She capered delightedly around, clapping her hands in front of her, but saw that he was watching her with

an unreadable expression on his face. Only when she
had come to an uncertain halt did he reply.

'I'm sorry, Caroline,' he retorted grimly. 'The last
thing in the world I intend to do is help you find that
plant.'

CHAPTER THREE

FOR fully ten seconds Caroline was stunned into silence. Then she found her voice.

'But why?' she demanded.

Adam folded his arms and stared at her unwinkingly.

'Because this whole thing may be nothing more than an elaborate hoax,' he replied. 'Oh, I grant you, it sounds convincing. Helping the poor kids with leukaemia—what could be a more persuasive argument? But I can't help suspecting that the whole thing is just a pack of lies you've cooked up for my benefit.'

The colour drained out of her face.

'But what possible reason would I have for lying about it?' she choked.

'If you're in league with Michael Barclay, then you'd have every reason in the world,' said Adam evenly. 'As you no doubt realise!'

'In league...?' she echoed in a baffled voice. 'What on earth are you talking about?'

'Oh, don't come the simple innocent with me!' he snapped. 'Do you seriously mean to tell me that you didn't know what kind of man you were dealing with in Michael Barclay? He may be an "awfully nice chap" as you say, but he's also a conman, a thief and a liar!'

'What?' cried Caroline, aghast. 'Whatever do you mean?'

Adam kicked a stray swimming-pool scoop impatiently out of his way and strode towards her. Then he gripped her by the shoulders.

'That painting which Michael Barclay sold to your museum was stolen from a sacred Aboriginal site on my land two years ago,' he said savagely. 'Barclay came out here posing as a harmless tourist, won the confidence

50

of the local Aborigines and was taken into the area where the sacred paintings are. OK? He headed off for Darwin and then doubled back. Once he was sure nobody was observing the area, he went out there with a diamond saw and hacked a large section out of a rock painting. It was worth hundreds of thousands of dollars in any museum collection of Aboriginal art, but as far as the Aborigines themselves were concerned it was utterly priceless and irreplaceable. We managed to track Barclay as far as Darwin, but he'd already boarded a plane for England. The last place he'd been sighted was a pub in Darwin, where he apparently went on a bender and boasted to a couple of people in the bar about what a terrific coup he'd pulled off. And not only that. He also swore blind that he'd be back one of these days to pick up the rest of the paintings. And there've been unconfirmed reports that he's been sighted in Darwin in the last couple of months.'

Caroline gaped.

'That's awful,' she said at last. 'But what's it got to do with me?'

Adam released his grip on her shoulders and let out a muffled curse.

'I don't know whether it's got anything to do with you,' he muttered. 'But I can't afford to take any chances on it. When I first met you, I thought you were just a tourist who'd been fool enough to break down on a back road that's hardly ever used. But now I find that you want to be taken to the one and only place where the fire lily plants grow—which just coincidentally happens to be the site where the sacred paintings are. Well, it sounds extremely suspicious to me. If Michael Barclay shows his face in these parts again, he knows damned well that I'll take him apart with my bare hands. So it would be very convenient for him to have a harmless-looking accomplice to do his dirty work, wouldn't it?'

Caroline's eyes filled with angry tears.

'So you're calling me a thief and a liar, are you?' she challenged.

Adam winced, but stood his ground.

'I'm not calling you anything,' he said. 'I'm simply telling you that I'll have to be very careful until I know what's going on here. And I must say the whole story sounds just a bit too pat. After all, how on earth did you know where to look for the fire lilies if Michael Barclay didn't send you here?'

Caroline caught her breath impatiently.

'I didn't know exactly,' she said. 'I still don't. What happened was that Terry Connor, our art curator, made a guess based on artistic style and geological evidence. And he just happened to be pretty accurate. Winnamurra Station is right in the centre of the area that he marked out for me on the map. But that doesn't make me a criminal!'

Adam sighed.

'Well, there's only one thing I can suggest,' he said. 'maybe you are completely genuine about this plant, but until I know that for sure I don't want you hanging around my land anywhere near those rock paintings. In my opinion, the people who have the best right to decide whether you should go near the site are the local Aboriginal tribe. Unfortunately they're semi-nomadic and some of them, including the tribal elders, are out on walkabout right now. But they should be back in about three weeks, so what I suggest is this. Why don't you let Danny Japulula drive you back to Darwin and book a room in a hotel for you? Then, when the tribal elders return, I'll tell them everything you've told me and they can decide whether to let you into the area to study the plants. Besides, that will give me time to check you out with the Darwin police and find out whether you really do have any association with Michael Barclay. What do you say?'

For a moment Caroline was so upset that she could say nothing at all. Then she took a deep breath and stared beseechingly at Adam.

'I don't want to go to Darwin,' she protested at last. 'You can't imagine how frustrating it would be to sit kicking my heels in a hotel room after I've come all this way to reach the outback. Anyway, I can't afford a hotel.'

'I'll pay for it,' offered Adam.

'And I don't want to take your money!' she added. 'Besides, I'd just be wasting my time in Darwin.'

'Now look here,' continued Adam, 'what's the hurry about getting out to see these fire lily plants? All right, it's July and they should be in bloom right now, but they won't produce seeds until the burning season, which doesn't arrive until August or September—usually late September with fire lilies. And then it's another two or three weeks until the seeds fall. So even if you could get to the site, what could you possibly do there?'

'I could collect some mature specimens!' she said. 'I might be able to take them back to Darwin and get them to set seed, especially now that I know they need fire.'

'I doubt it!' retorted Adam sceptically. 'They probably wouldn't even survive the transplanting. Anyway, in my opinion, you'd be a damned fool if you went out there right now, trampling around near the sacred paintings and upsetting the Aborigines, when you might get them a hundred per cent behind you just by waiting and asking their permission. If you're genuine about these fire lily plants, I'm sure the tribal elders will let you collect samples of them when they're good and ready. But it will be when they choose, not when you do. And if that means you have to sit and wait in Darwin for the next three weeks, then that's what you'll damned well do.'

'Can't you give me permission to go to the site?' asked Caroline. 'After all, it is on your land, presumably.'

Adam shook his head slowly.

'That's not the way I see it,' he said. 'The Aborigines believe that the land owns the people, not the other way round. And while it may be mine legally, I respect their traditions too much to offend them. So I'm simply not prepared to let you go trampling around out there near the sacred paintings and upsetting the local people. They feel the same way about their sacred sites that you would about a cathedral or the grave of somebody you loved. If you had any sense of decency at all, you wouldn't even think of going there without their approval. Unless, of course, it's the paintings you're really after anyway.'

Caroline sank into a chair and groaned. Coming hard on the heels of her ordeal with the jeep, this attack seemed totally unbearable.

'I am not after the paintings!' she exclaimed. 'All I want is the fire lilies, but it seems as if everything possible is going wrong. I've wrecked my jeep and you seem to think I'm some kind of international art thief. But I won't give up! Even if you send me to Darwin, I'll come back as soon as I possibly can.'

Adam stared at her with a baffled look.

'Why does it matter so much to you?' he asked.

She tried to marshal her thoughts, but found that fatigue was making her head spin.

'Have you ever seen a child with leukaemia?' she demanded at last.

Her eyes rose to his—grey, candid and burning with fervour.

'No, I can't say I have,' he admitted unwillingly.

'Well, I have,' retorted Caroline. 'And it's heartbreaking—not only for the child, but for everyone who cares about him. Just take a look at this.'

She delved into her pocket and produced a colour photo of a three-year old boy with a completely bald head, a cheeky grin and mischievous brown eyes. Her lips quivered as she handed it across to Adam. He gazed at it in silence for a long moment, then passed it back to her.

'Who is he?' he asked.

'He was my godson,' she replied, 'Andrew Clive Mathieson. He had chemotherapy for nearly a year, but unfortunately he was one of the kids who didn't make it. He died two days before Christmas last year.'

Their eyes met and held.

'I'm sorry,' said Adam curtly.

Caroline grimaced.

'Well, there's nothing I can do for Andy now,' she responded with a defiant lift of her chin. 'But there are other kids, Adam. Other kids who might be in with a chance if I can get those plants and give them to the right pharmaceutical people. And I have a terrible sense of time ticking away. All right, I accept that I can't collect the plants without permission from the tribal elders, but I wish I didn't have to go back to Darwin. At least if I were here, I could swing into action the minute they came back.'

Adam stared moodily at her.

'I'll say this for you,' he remarked, 'you don't give up easily once you've set your heart on something. All right, Caroline. If I can't persuade you to wait in Darwin until the tribal elders return, there's only one other thing I can suggest.'

'What's that?' she asked.

'You can come with me. I'm due to go out on the range for ten days or so to mend some fences along my northern boundary. And I've got breeding stock to inspect, so I could stretch the trip to last two or three weeks. If you come with me, I could keep you under my eye. That way Danny can give us a call on the radio as soon as the elders return. What do you say?'

Caroline was taken aback. Two weeks out on the range with Adam Fletcher? How on earth would she cope with the enforced intimacy of being alone with him for so long? She stole a hasty glance at him and was suddenly conscious of his immense physical power, of the hard, muscular thrust of his thighs under his grey trousers, of the hair that glinted like sunlight on his tanned arms.

Against her will she felt desire swell through her like a bursting wave. Colour rushed into her cheeks.

'Couldn't I just stay here at the homestead while you're away?' she asked in a stifled voice.

Adam stared at her suspiciously.

'No, you couldn't!' he retorted. 'If you are working for Barclay, he's probably given you directions about where to find the paintings, so I don't want you sneaking off the site as soon as I'm gone. And even if you really are a harmless botanist, you're too wet behind the ears to be trusted alone. You'd probably go out looking for plants and get lost again.'

'I won't——' she began, but Adam's face was implacable.

'You're damned right you won't!' he said forcefully. 'Because you won't have the opportunity. You've only got two choices, you know. Now which is it going to be? Are you going back to Darwin or are you coming with me?'

She hesitated, staring into those keen blue eyes. Then she made her decision.

'I'll come with you,' she said.

Adam took her hands and drew her to her feet.

'In that case, you ought to get some sleep,' he advised. 'I'm planning on an early start tomorrow while it's still relatively cool.'

'All right,' she agreed, nervously trying to withdraw her hands from his.

He released her fingers without protest, but he looked at her warily.

'Why are you so jumpy?' he asked. 'Is something bothering you?'

'N-no,' she lied.

'Of course,' he continued, 'if you're trying to trick me over these paintings, then you have good reason to be nervous. But if you're genuine, Caroline, you have no need to fear going into the outback with me. I promise you that.'

His lips brushed her cheek lightly.

'Goodnight,' he said.

As she made her way to bed, Caroline felt as if her face were on fire from that casual touch. She wasn't even sure what it meant. Was it a warning or a reassurance, or both? Whatever Adam's intention, he had aroused such turmoil deep inside her that she found herself quite unable to sleep, in spite of her exhaustion. Her tired brain swam with images of Adam on camel back, Adam swimming naked in a rock pool, Adam looking stern and angry as he described the theft of the paintings. Then she remembered that momentary warmth in his eyes as he had kissed her and a deep, pulsing heat seemed to throb through her veins. With an exasperated sigh, she punched her pillow and turned over. What she was experiencing was a totally new sensation. Certainly she had never felt anything of the kind for her husband. Staring sightlessly into the darkness, she let her mind run back to the day she had first met Jeremy.

It had been one of those perfect English summer days when the pale gold sunlight seemed to pour into the landscape like sparkling white wine. Every tree and shrub in her father's garden was bursting with fresh green foliage and flowers rioted in the borders against the mellow red brick walls. Lupins and campions and sneezeweed and bellflowers released a heady perfume that drifted through the garden, enticing visitors to crouch and sniff and exclaim. In the centre of the velvety south lawn under the shade of the massive oak trees, Caroline's stepmother was in her element, directing operations like a policeman in a busy intersection. The midsummer garden party at Monkton Hall was always the highlight of her year, and this time there was not even a drop of rain to spoil her triumph. In fact the only cloud on her horizon was her gawky eighteen-year-old stepdaughter Caroline, mooning around on the fringes of the crowd, blushing when anybody spoke to her.

'Oh, do stop looking so gormless and make yourself useful, Caroline!' cried Susan Faircroft, impatiently thrusting a tray into her hands. 'Here, take some wine over to Jeremy Hetherington and introduce yourself. He's the dark-haired chap over by the sundial, talking to your father. A stockbroker from London, charming fellow. Now off you go!'

And with a brisk push she unwittingly launched Caroline on a path that was to lead to marriage.

Looking back on it now, ten years later, Caroline could not repress a shudder.

'Oh, Jeremy, why did it all have to end so badly?' she whispered. 'I thought all my dreams had come true when I met you.'

Susan had been right about one thing: Jeremy's charm. In spite of being thirty years old and urbane enough to take his pick of the women present, he had chosen to flirt harmlessly with the shy, immature Caroline all afternoon and even to kiss her in the shrubbery behind the summerhouse. Murmuring husky words of endearment, he even threaded a handful of tiny Cecile Brunner roses through her tumbled brown hair. Caroline found the whole experience utterly enchanting. In spite of her model-girl looks, or perhaps because of them, she had never received much attention from youths of her own age. Eighteen- and nineteen-year-olds were intimidated by her cool elegance and her shyness was often misinterpreted as aloofness. Unbelievably, Jeremy's kiss was the first she had ever had from a man, and it went to her head like wine. The night of the garden party she lay awake, flushed and exalted, for hours, clasping in her hands a heavy book in which Jeremy's roses were lovingly pressed between sheets of clean white paper.

Even Caroline was not so naïve as to expect anything to come of that single day's magic, and she had been astonished and thrilled two months later when Jeremy arrived at her rooms in a Cambridge women's college and whisked her off to lunch. Not knowing that he had planned the outing with another girl and been stood up at the last moment, Caroline was dazzled to find that he had a champagne picnic packed in a wicker hamper, complete with chocolates and flowers. A couple of hours spent lazing under willow trees followed by a peaceful afternoon on the river did their work. By the end of the day Caroline was head over heels in love, and Jeremy, piqued by her unexpected resistance to anything more than kissing, had issued an invitation to lunch the following Sunday. His hunter's instincts were aroused, and he was determined to possess her.

As it turned out, it was a pursuit which was to take him more than two years. Jeremy was incredulous to learn that Caroline had some extraordinarily old-fashioned notions about love, sex and marriage, and he began to devote his considerable charm to wearing her down. Caroline remained adamant. She was certain that sex without commitment would only make her miserable, so it must be marriage or nothing. Incredibly, Jeremy found himself so obsessed with the idea of possessing her cool, statuesque beauty that he capitulated. Two years after he had first met her, they became engaged, and on her twenty-first birthday the relationship was finally consummated.

Caroline had expected it to be the most wonderful moment of her life. Instead it was pure disaster. Her mother had thrown a magnificent party for her and, when the last guest had left, Jeremy had coaxed her to come back to his flat. There he had abandoned all pretence of charm or civility and announced belligerently that it was time he had his rights. Too late Caroline realised how heavily he had been drinking at her party and tried to leave, but he blocked the front door with his body and then hauled her off to bed. What followed was barbaric. Ten minutes later Caroline, sobbing in bewilderment, was lying huddled miserably with a sheet over her head while Jeremy hurled abuse at her for her frigidity.

It might have been best if they had parted at once, but the following day Jeremy arrived with flowers and apologies. He assured her that everything would improve once she was used to it. But it didn't. They went ahead with the marriage, and soon life was a hideous round of unsuccessful attempts at lovemaking, violent quarrels and frozen silences. All through the first two years of their relationship Jeremy had amused himself with women who were more accommodating than Caroline, and now he simply resumed the habit. But although he was potent enough with them, he now found to his rage and dismay that it was not only Caroline who had difficulties with sex. After several humiliating failures with her, he turned angrily to drinking, which only compounded their problems. Shortly after Caroline's twenty-fourth birthday, he announced that he was running off with her best friend, and added that she had only herself to blame because of her frigidity. A year later they were divorced.

At first Caroline wept violently into her pillow every night, haunted by the fear that Jeremy was right and that the entire fiasco was all her fault. But after a few months she slowly realised that it was a relief not to have Jeremy's blustering, ill-tempered presence in her home. She was lonely, but she could cope with that, and she threw herself into her work with a dedication that left her no time for a social life. By now she had a good job with a leading London museum and plenty of opportunities to meet other men. But there was nobody who had ever stirred her senses in any way until the moment when Adam Fletcher suddenly exploded into her life with all the force of a nuclear warhead.

She was stunned by the violent and contradictory emotions that Adam awoke in her. At first she had simply disliked him. Tough, resourceful, devoted to the land and contemptuous of inexperienced outsiders, he had been absolutely blistering in his scorn for her when she had wrecked the jeep. But, once she saw how close to death she had been, his reaction no longer seemed so unforgivable. And perhaps he needed to be harsh to survive in this grim environment. Yet even his harshness seemed to be balanced by flashes of unexpected good humour and kindness. He had been an attentive host and, in spite of his suspicions about Caroline, he had not forced her to return to Darwin. It was just a pity that such impassable barriers had already been flung up between them. If only the drama of the stolen paintings hadn't come between them, perhaps they could have been quite good friends. But as Caroline slipped into sleep, she couldn't help wondering whether friendship was all that she really wanted from Adam...

It was shortly after six o'clock when she woke the following morning. Opening the french doors, she padded out on to the screened veranda outside her bedroom. The sky was a deep, cloudless blue and the air still felt fresh and crisp with no hint of the intense heat that midday would bring. Down below she saw Adam peering under the bonnet of a four-wheel-drive vehicle. He was dressed in khaki shorts, an old army shirt and heavy leather boots and his head was shaded by a battered Akubra cowboy hat. As she watched, he straightened up, raised a dipstick in the air and frowned critically at it. Then he caught sight of her and gave her a casual salute.

'You'd better come and get some breakfast,' he shouted. 'I'll be ready to head off in half an hour and I don't fancy waiting around while you touch up your lipstick.'

Caroline showered and dressed in record time and even managed to dab on some lipstick before she bolted into the kitchen. She found that Adam was already in occupation, leaning on the countertop and whistling as he waited for something to heat in the microwave oven.

'There's cereal and fruit juice on the table,' he said pleasantly, 'Eggs and bacon in the frying pan. And doughnuts in the microwave. What would you like?'

'Juice and cereal, please,' replied Caroline, sitting down.

'Well, help yourself,' urged Adam with a wave of a spatula. 'I'm having everything.'

In a moment he was sitting opposite her and setting down a plate laden with three eggs and about half a pound of bacon. He reached for the jug of orange juice.

'Nice day, isn't it?' he said cheerfully. 'Makes you feel glad to be alive.'

He offered her some juice, then applied himself to the serious business of demolishing the mountain of food in front of him. Caroline ate more slowly, savouring the fruity coolness of the juice and the crunchy texture of the cornflakes. Now that Adam had agreed to help her, she was far more conscious of his good points. Not only was he handsome and capable, but very obliging as well. She vowed silently that this expedition would be as harmonious as she could possibly make it. If Adam could be so gracious about pleasing her, the least she could do was to be equally gracious in return. As soon as she finished her fragrant black coffee, she got to her feet and helped him to load the dishwasher. In spite of the lack of chatter, she could not help thinking how companionable it was to share this homely task with somebody. Even the clutter of Adam's kitchen with its pile of bills on a spike by the telephone and a scattering of farm magazines seemed oddly appealing. As soon as we get back, she thought, I'll give this place a really good scrub and make it look decent.

'Ready to go?' asked Adam, turning on the dishwasher.

'Whenever you are!' agreed Caroline blithely.

Her good humour stayed with her as they left the house and climbed into the jeep. She was humming softly as Adam opened the rear door of the vehicle and stowed

her pack inside. To her surprise she saw that every
available inch was crammed full of equipment. Large
plastic containers of water, cartons of tinned food,
groundsheets, sleeping bags, axes, ropes, a tool kit, a
first aid kit, a Coleman lantern and some fire-blackened
cooking pots all jostled for space, along with a roll of
fencing wire, a bin full of tools and a large motorbike.

'My goodness!' she exclaimed. 'What a lot of stuff!
It looks as if you mean to live out there.'

Adam shrugged.

'Well, there won't be any shops if I've forgotten anything,' he pointed out. 'Now come on, let's get moving.'

As they bumped down the red dust track that led under
overhanging green peppercorn trees, a cluster of white
bungalow-style houses came into view on their left. Close
by was a labyrinth of wooden stockyards where dust rose
gold and choking in the sunlight and the air rang with
the bellowing of cattle and the crack of stockwhips.
Dark-skinned men in checked shirts, jeans and cowboy
hats moved among the teeming throng of beasts, wielding
their branding irons. The reek of singed hides and
pungent droppings wafted through the open window, and
Caroline wrinkled her nose and recoiled.

'There must be hundreds of cattle there!' she exclaimed in amazement.

'Yes, it's pretty busy this time of year,' agreed Adam
laconically. 'As a matter of fact, we're generally flat out
the whole time from April to September, what with
mustering, branding, calving and the whole works. It
never really lets up much until the wet season sets in
around November.'

'Can you really spare the time to take me out for two
or three weeks, then?' asked Caroline uncomfortably.

'No,' replied Adam. 'But you haven't given me a whole
lot of choice, have you?'

She quailed. Feeling as if she were running out of conversation at a cocktail party, she gazed despairingly

around for inspiration, and saw half a dozen Aboriginal children perched on a wooden fence and waving.

'How many people actually live here?' she asked in surprise.

'Twenty-three,' said Adam. 'No, hang on, Maisie Yunupingu had a baby boy last month, so I guess it's twenty-four now. I have five permanent staff with their families and this time of year, while the cattle season is on, I employ another eight or ten stockmen. And of course there are the people who still live a tribal lifestyle and wander on and off the station. Some of them do casual work for me from time to time.'

'You must have quite a big property, then,' said Caroline.

'Big enough,' agreed Adam. 'About eight hundred thousand acres. So it's a fair-sized operation to run. Now hold on to your seat while we go over this cattle grid, because it feels like working on a jack hammer.'

Caroline's teeth vibrated in her head as they drove slowly over the spaced bars which allowed vehicles to pass, but discouraged cattle. Almost at once, they found themselves in a brilliantly coloured landscape where red dust and brilliant blue sky were softened only by the silver-grey tufts of spinifex and the leathery foliage of hakeas and eucalypts. Stretching out in her seat, she gave a long, luxurious sigh.

'Tell me about the station, how long your family's had it, what you want to do with it, all that sort of thing,' she urged.

Adam's eyes kindled.

'Well, we've had it a good while,' he said. 'My great-grandfather first settled here around the turn of the century, but he never could make a real go of the place. Back in those days most of the pastoral properties went broke because of disease and ticks. There's a real problem with parasites in the tropics, and the trouble was that the kind of cattle they were running just weren't suited to the conditions up here. When my grandfather took over, he had to supplement the income from the property by going off shooting crocodiles in Arnhem Land, so my dad was the first one who really worked the place systematically. He brought in a whole lot of Brahmins and encouraged them to breed and I've done the same thing.'

'Brahmins?' echoed Caroline in a baffled voice. 'I thought they were Hindu priests!'

Adam gave a hoot of laughter.

'They may well be,' he retorted. 'But they're also a really fine breed of cattle that can tolerate extremely harsh conditions and are very resistant to ticks. Look, there are some Brahmins!'

His muscular brown arm brushed past her as he pointed across her body and out through the passenger window. She was conscious of a faint flutter in her throat at the realisation of his nearness, then she obediently followed his pointing finger. Grazing placidly amid the clumps of spinifex were half a dozen pale gold cattle with long ears, mild dreamy faces and pendulous dewlaps of skin hanging from their throats.

'Oh, aren't they sweet?' cried Caroline.

'Nice-looking beasts,' agreed Adam. 'I've imported two hundred and fifty females and twenty bulls in the last couple of years, so when it's all up and running I intend to have one of the finest cattle studs in the Territory. And what's more, I'll do it without over-grazing the place and wrecking the land. You know, it's heartbreaking country up here, tough and harsh and un-yielding, but it's full of magnificent surprises too. And if you really fall under its spell, everything else in the world is just a poor second-best to it.'

His blue eyes brightened as he stared through the windscreen at the red-gold landscape that enveloped them. And as she watched the rapt look on his face, Caroline felt an obscure sense of pain and vulnerability stab through her. You weren't just describing the country, Adam, she thought uncomfortably. That was a perfect portrait of you—tough and harsh and unyielding and, no doubt, full of magnificent surprises. But you needn't think I'll fall under your spell.

'How long till we reach our campsite?' she asked abruptly.

'Three or four hours,' he replied. 'We'll be off the track soon, and the going gets pretty rough.'

That was an understatement, thought Caroline several hours later. She had been bruised and jolted along rocky ridges and over dry creek beds until she no longer had the faintest idea where she was going or where she had come from. She thought they were heading east, but since the sun in this odd part of the world seemed to travel the wrong way across the sky she could not even be sure of that. Her head ached, her throat was dry and choked with dust and her clothes were plastered to her body with sweat. When Adam finally brought the jeep to a halt under a vast, spreading gum tree beside a rocky pool, she had never been so grateful in her life. Unfolding her cramped limbs, she hobbled stiffly away from the vehicle and stretched herself thoroughly. Wincing as she massaged the back of her neck, she climbed back into the jeep and rummaged in her bag until she found a bottle of aspirin. She shook two tablets into her palm, took a swift gulp of water from her screw-top bottle and shuddered. Adam was already hauling equipment out of the back of the vehicle, but he threw her a swift, measuring look.

'You OK?' he demanded brusquely.

'Yes, of course,' replied Caroline, rallying. 'I'll help you make camp in a moment.'

'Don't worry about it,' insisted Adam. 'You just sit down in the shade and get over the trip. You'd probably be more of a hindrance than a help anyway.'

Caroline felt a surge of annoyance at that, but she let it pass, particularly since he at once pulled out a folding chair and table which he set in the shade of the eucalyptus tree. Without a word, he also brought out an ice-

box, pulled out a can of icy cold Coke and put it in front
of her. By the time Caroline had gulped down the last
of the frosty, tingling liquid, he had already hacked down
four substantial branches to act as supports for a make-
shift shelter.

'Aren't you going to stop and have a drink?' she asked.
'In a while,' he replied. 'I want to finish this first.'

Before long he had built quite an impressive shelter
with a roof made from green canvas groundsheets and
even a small awning as added protection from the sun.
He did stop long enough to gulp down a soft drink, but
almost at once he was back at work unpacking supplies.
In less than two hours the camp was complete down to
the last detail, including a cooking-pit downwind of the
shelter with a stick of firewood beside it, a Bioloo set
inside a small green tent and a shower contraption
hanging over the branch of a gum tree. Inside the shelter,
Adam's preparations were equally elaborate, with such
comforts as feather pillows, air mattresses, Rich Asmara
coffee beans and a gas-operated refrigerator. Obviously
whenever Adam Fletcher camped out he did it in style.
Yet it was not until he had inspected everything that he
finally set down his tools and took a can of cold beer
out of the ice chest.

'Would you like some lunch?' he asked Caroline.

By now the aspirin had taken effect and she was
anxious to be helpful.

'I'll make it,' she offered, and was soon busy setting
out plates of cold ham and salad.

They ate in companionable silence, then Adam rose
to his feet.

'I'd better take the bike out and start checking the
boundary fence now,' he announced. 'Will you be all
right on your own for a few hours?'

'Yes, of course,' agreed Caroline briskly. 'I'll have a
look at some of the plants down by the pool.'

'Fine,' said Adam. 'Just watch where you walk. There
aren't any crocodiles in this area, but there are quite a

lot of poisonous snakes, and you could find the odd
scorpion too.'

Caroline swallowed hard. Snakes? Scorpions? As
Adam loaded up the back of the motorbike, she had to
fight a cowardly urge to beg him to take her along too.
Except that if she did he would have no room for the
tote box full of fencing wire and tools, which would make
the whole excursion pointless. His blue eyes watched hers
with an unholy expression of amusement as if he were
reading her thoughts with no difficulty at all.

'Sure you can manage?' he asked with a hint of
mockery.

'Yes!' she insisted fiercely. 'I'll enjoy myself.'

'All right. I'll leave a CB radio with you. If you have
any trouble, just call me and I'll come straight back. I
won't be more than a mile or two away.'

For the first half-hour, Caroline was almost rigid with
terror, glancing nervously down at the ground as she
cleared the lunch dishes and washed up. But after a while,
when no scorpions or snakes materialised, she slowly
began to relax and even risked a cautious walk down
towards the pool. With her trowel she dug up some of
the plants that were growing there and took them back
to the shelter. One of the ferns seemed particularly interesting, so she set it in an acrylic tumbler full of water
and began to draw it carefully. Although the air was like
a hot blast on her skin, the awning cast a welcome shade,
and she poured herself a cool drink of mineral water
from the refrigerator. With a little experimenting, she
soon discovered that a wet T-shirt and a wet hat were
as effective as air-conditioning. The cicadas shrilled
loudly, an intense, aromatic fragrance wafted into the
air around the gum tree, the sky was a flawless cobalt
blue, and the only thing Caroline had to do was sit and
draw plants. To her surprise, she realised that she was
feeling very happy.

It was almost sunset when Adam returned, plastered
with red dust and sweat and looking like a wild man.

He greeted her with a casual hail, drank a large cold beer and headed for the shower. When he came back five minutes later, he was completely transformed in clean denim jeans and a checked shirt with his hair combed. And a subtle tang of French aftershave clung to his skin.

'Would you like a shower too?' he suggested. 'I didn't think to mention it to you before.'

'Yes, please!' she agreed gratefully.

'Put something warmer on when you finish,' he shouted after her. 'It'll be cold once the sun goes down.'

There was no screen around the shower and Caroline felt self-conscious about stripping naked, but Adam completely ignored her. Out of the corner of her eye, she could see him making a pyramid of kindling for a campfire, so she undressed and turned on the water. Instinctively she flinched, expecting it to be cold, but the sun had heated it and it was quite warm. Unfortunately the container was small, so the water supply ran out just as she finished rinsing her hair. All the same, she felt pleasantly refreshed as she scrambled into jeans and a shirt and towelled her head briskly. As she walked back towards the shelter, she saw that the sun was setting in a lavish blaze of gold and crimson.

'Isn't that magnificent?' she breathed, halting and lifting her face to the sky.

Adam had the fire crackling brightly and was busy snapping lengths of wood over his knee, but he also paused and looked up.

'Yes, it is,' he agreed. 'That was one of the reasons I moved back to the Territory—to watch the sunsets.'

Caroline was startled by this simple statement. For all his tough, virile nature, she was beginning to suspect that Adam was far more complex than she had originally thought.

'You really have a bond with this country, don't you?' she asked as she sat down in a camp chair.

'Yes,' he agreed. 'It's harsh country and it doesn't suit everyone, but I belong here. I felt stifled in the cities, but out here I'm free. Master of my own destiny, I suppose you could say.'

There was a hint of self-mockery in his tone, but she found his words oddly moving. Only a man who was utterly convinced of his own power would ever have the courage to make his destiny in such a lonely, primitive environment. Seeing his muscular figure outlined against the blazing sky, she felt a surge of unwilling excitement flare through her. It was all she could do not to move forward and touch him.

'May I help you cook dinner?' she asked hastily.

Adam shrugged.

'Everything's under control,' he replied. 'And you can have anything you like, as long as it's barbecued steak and baked potatoes. But I can't start cooking until the fire dies down a bit so that we have some decent coals.'

Once the sun slipped below the horizon, night fell swiftly like a dark blue curtain and the air chilled noticeably. By now the fire was roaring vigorously and showers of orange sparks fizzed into the air like fireworks when Adam poked it with a stick.

'Let's have a drink while we wait for it to settle,' he suggested.

He disappeared inside the shelter and, to Caroline's amazement, soon returned with a Campari and soda for her, complete with ice and a twist of lemon and a Scotch on the rocks for himself. She took a slow, luxurious sip and sighed dreamily.

'I call that miraculous,' she murmured. 'However did you manage it?'

Adam chuckled throatily.

'You can manage anything if you're really determined,' he told her. 'And I've been swallowing dust all afternoon, so I think I deserve something decent now.'

'How did the fencing go?' she asked.

They began to chat casually, and she told him about her afternoon's work and showed him her drawings. He talked about the difficulty of preventing stock from straying into Arnhem Land, the huge Aboriginal reserve to the north, which white people could only enter by permit and where Aboriginal hunters and gatherers still lived in Stone Age style. It was a fascinating conversation and ranged over everything from Aboriginal myths to the best way to play a didgeridoo. When Adam rose to check the fire, Caroline gave a sigh of contentment.

'You know, Adam,' she said, 'I'm so glad I came here. I'm really starting to feel it's the adventure of a lifetime, in spite of what everybody told me before I left.'

'What did they tell you?' asked Adam, raising his eyebrows quizzically.

'That I was stark, raving mad,' she replied. 'That the whole project was a waste of time.'

'You must have convinced somebody that the project was useful or you wouldn't have been given funding for it,' he remarked.

Caroline pulled a face.

'I didn't get any funding,' she admitted.

'What? Then how did you manage to finance the trip?' A rueful smile lit her face.

'By a bout of pure insanity,' she confessed. 'I did try to get funds from some of the research institutes, but they all said it was too chancy. So I sold my car and some government bonds that my grandmother had left me and took six months' leave without pay from my job. Then I simply flew to Australia.'

'That's very brave of you,' said Adam with respect.

'Not really. I was scared stiff. I'm not really the adventurous type, you see, but my godson's illness gave me a dreadful jolt. I cared about Andy almost as much as if he'd been my own child, so when I had the chance to do something I had to take it.'

Adam's blue eyes were narrowed thoughtfully.

'You say you cared about him almost as much as if he were your own child,' he murmured. 'And yet last night you told me that you didn't want children, that you only wanted a career. Isn't that rather a contradiction?'

Caroline flushed, taken aback by his shrewdness.

'It's not important, surely?' she protested defensively.

'Isn't it?' he queried. 'I think you can tell a lot about people if you know what they want. Anyway, why didn't you want children? Was it just because of your career? Or did your husband influence you?'

'Please don't talk to me about Jeremy,' said Caroline in a tense voice. 'It's over now. It's finished.'

'Is it?' demanded Adam sceptically. 'You know, it's interesting, Caroline. Whenever your husband's name is mentioned, you get a haunted look in your eyes. I've seen that sort of look on the faces of refugees. Sometimes it's the memory of unbearable love, other times of unbearable pain. Either way, it means that the past isn't really over for them. It still has the power to destroy their future. I can't help wondering whether that's what's happening to you.'

'Don't be silly,' she said unsteadily. 'Look, don't you think those coals are ready now?'

The coals were ready and, to her relief, Adam dropped his merciless probing and began instructing her in the art of bush cookery. Before long their earlier light-heartedness was recaptured. He showed her how to wrap potatoes in foil and set them to roast in the hot red embers and, with great hilarity, he gave her a lesson in making damper, the bushman's substitute for bread. By the time she was covered in splashes of sticky white dough and giggling helplessly, they both had to admit that the lesson was a failure.

'You'll never make a stockman, my girl,' he grumbled, elbowing her aside. 'Go and wash your hands and let the master chef take over.'

Soon the delicious aroma of baking potatoes filled the air and Adam set the thick, juicy steaks to grill over the coals, while Caroline tossed a salad. The damper emerged at last, crusty and golden-brown with no signs of damage, and they both ate ravenously. But Caroline had her revenge when they reached the pudding. Adam's only offering was tinned peaches, and she offered to make some French pancakes. Cooking over a campfire proved trickier than she expected, but after a couple of burnt fingers and a loud 'Ow!' she soon mastered the art. The pancakes were a great success, crisp and thin, doused with lemon juice and caster sugar and with a perfect lacy brown finish. Adam ate five.

'I'm only doing this so I won't hurt your feelings,' he said with a wicked glint in his eye, as he reached for his sixth.

'You lying beast!' protested Caroline, snatching the plate indignantly out of his reach and leaping to her feet.

With a growl of laughter he leapt after her and pursued her round the fire. She tried to hold the plate above her head, but Adam responded by tickling her unmercifully. Giggling and squirming, she doubled up.

'Ow, stop it, stop it! I'm desperately ticklish. Don't! Don't!'

Suddenly everything seemed to stand still. Caroline noticed that the plate had fallen unheeded to the ground, but it hardly seemed to matter. For at that moment a strange, wild yearning flooded through her with such force that she felt her legs trembling. Instinctively she clutched at Adam for support and saw the expression on his face change. His eyes blazed, dark and unreadable in the firelight, then his fingers threaded through her silky hair and his mouth moved urgently down to hers.

CHAPTER FOUR

ADAM'S kisses were warm, sensual, dangerously tormenting, and Caroline found herself responding with an ardour that shocked her. Reason could not still the ache that was unfolding in her loins and throbbing through her entire body, making her breath come faster and her heart hammer furiously. Winding her arms around Adam's neck, she kissed him back, and felt a thrill of arousal as his grip tightened on her. His hand touched the base of her spine, moving in a slow, caressing circle that pressed her against his hard, masculine warmth. An involuntary whimper escaped her at that quivering contact and her lips parted softly. She heard his sharp, uneven breathing and felt the exquisite pressure of his hands moving rhythmically over her flesh. His touch was unbearably arousing and, as if of its own accord, her body arched provocatively against his, glorying in his virile strength and possession. Then a small voice inside her whispered, 'Don't be such a fool, Caroline!' With a sudden gasp, she pushed him away.

'I'm sorry!' she gabbled. 'I shouldn't...I didn't mean...'

He stared at her in exasperation.

'Do I really disgust you so much?' he demanded.

Her lower lip quivered dangerously and she caught it between her teeth, fighting to hold back tears.

'It's not to do with you!' she said in an agonised voice. 'It's to do with me...and things...that happened in the past. Things that have nothing to do with you, Adam!'

'Your precious husband, Jeremy, I suppose?' Adam's voice was scathing.

'Yes!' choked Caroline.

She was shaking all over now, holding her arms tightly around her slender body, as if to stop herself from falling to pieces.

'Why did you break up with him?' demanded Adam brutally. 'Did you leave him or did he leave you?'

'Adam, please! Just drop it, will you? It's nothing to do with you!'

'Answer me!' he insisted.

She became aware that his muscular brown arms were around her and looked down with a dazed expression on her face. Gripping his fingers, she tried to pry them loose, but she might as well have tugged at steel cables.

'Let me go!' she gasped. 'You're hurting me! Adam...'

'Answer me!' he repeated, thrusting his face so close to hers that she could see the individual lashes around his blue eyes.

'He left me.'

'Why?'

His voice was harsh, pitiless, demanding, and it seemed easier to give in than to fight. A tremor went through her as she replied.

'He ran off with my best friend,' she said on an upward, wavering intonation, then burst into tears.

Adam swore under his breath and then gathered her into his arms and rocked her.

'But you're still in love with the bastard, aren't you?' he demanded.

Caroline hesitated. Her eyes were stinging and her breath came in brief, shuddering gulps. For a moment she contemplated telling him the whole sorry saga, but even the thought of it made her cringe. It was all too raw, too painful, too humiliating. Better to let him think his guess was right. Perhaps then he would leave her alone and this dangerous attraction she felt for him would subside.

'Yes,' she said dully. And then with more urgency, 'Yes! Yes! I'm still in love with Jeremy!'

Adam was holding her so tightly that she felt as if her ribs would crack. His breath stirred her hair and a quiver of emotion ran through her at the sudden fierce pressure of his lips. Then he held her away at arm's length so that he could gaze fiercely into her tear-sodden grey eyes.

'You little fool!' he exclaimed angrily. 'Can't you see that a man like that isn't worth wasting your tears on? Why don't you just let go of the memories and start afresh?'

Caroline swallowed hard.

'I can't,' she replied bleakly. 'I just can't escape from it.'

And that much at least is true, she thought, blinking back the tears and staring hard at a buttonhole on Adam's shirt. His hands massaged her back, sending waves of soothing comfort through her entire body so that she made a small, involuntary sound in the back of her throat. Clutching the lapels of his shirt, she looked up into his exasperated face.

'Adam,' she begged, 'please. You must realise now that it's a big mistake for us to do this. Don't you see that?'

Adam gave a grim smile.

'No, I don't,' he said. 'What I see is that there's a very powerful physical attraction between us and for some reason you want to pretend that it doesn't exist. Well, I can't see the sense in that. We're both free agents, aren't we?'

Caroline made a small, helpless gesture with her hands as if she were warding off a blow.

'I suppose so,' she admitted despairingly. 'But that doesn't mean that we have to give in to some purely physical urge. If we're going to stay out here together, couldn't you just agree not to touch me?'

Putting his fingers under her chin, he raised her face to his and kissed her again, slowly and lingeringly. In spite of the tension between them, his touch still had the power to move her profoundly. To her surprise, Caroline felt a deep fountain of longing spring up inside her as his mouth met hers. His lips moved sensually on hers, brushing, teasing, coaxing, until a breathless tingling sensation began to uncoil inside her and she let out a long, uneven sigh. Then he reluctantly drew his mouth away from hers.

'You can't have guarantees of safety, Caroline,' he growled. 'Life just doesn't offer them, and neither do I. But I will promise you one thing. Whatever is going to happen between us, I won't rush it. And while you're out here in the bush, you're going to have the most interesting time I can possibly give you.'

In the two weeks that followed Adam was true to his word. Each day brought a wealth of new experiences, and if it had not been for the acute emotional tension between them Caroline would have enjoyed every moment. As it was, she felt as if she were suffering some exquisitely refined form of torture. Never before in her life had she been thrown into a situation of such intense intimacy with anyone. Even when her relationship with Jeremy was at its worst point, there had always been other people around to defuse the stress. Here there was nobody. Not even a postman or a shop assistant. Just herself and Adam alone in a vast, primeval continent, as if the rest of the human race had mysteriously vanished from the planet. It gave her an eerie feeling sometimes, especially since it left her so dependent on Adam's knowledge and goodwill for her very survival.

His bond with the land was almost uncanny. For the first few days he worked like a demon to finish the repairs on the boundary fence, but after that he spent his time showing Caroline the countryside with equal energy. Although they returned each night to their base camp, during the daylight they ranged widely both on foot and in the jeep. Determined to show her as much as possible, Adam took her to rocky gorges where waterfalls gushed into green, sunlit pools and fishbone ferns clung pre-

cariously to the cliffsides. He guided her to escarpments
as rugged and boulder-strewn as any quarry, where the
sky overhead was such an intense, dazzling indigo that
it hurt her eyes to look at it. He showed her inland
waterways where crocodiles lay sunning themselves on
the muddy banks with their tiny eyes and cruel reptilian
teeth clearly visible. One memorable day he even drove
her the fifty miles or so to the coast and led her along
a flat, gleaming white beach against the jade-blue water
of the Gulf of Carpentaria. And all the time he was
showing her around, he was busy teaching her.

Although he did not have the theoretical training in
biology that Caroline had, his practical knowledge of
the plants and animals of the region was immense. And
it was all linked to the need for survival. He taught her
to recognise the grey-green casuarina trees on the coast
which indicated the presence of underground water
behind the sand dunes. He taught her how to find fresh-
water mussels under the reeds in running water, how to
dig in the dry red dust for edible honey ants, how to
pound grass seeds and prepare them as food. Before long
she began to see the landscape through Adam's eyes as
a treasure-house full of riches, a vast larder teeming with
food at every season. Her head reeled with the details
of salmon, bream, turtles, ducks, wild geese, billygoat
plums, macadamia nuts, and more roots and berries than
she had ever imagined. She used up every roll of film
she had brought with her and filled three notebooks with
her jottings. And each evening when they returned from
their wanderings she would sit watching the sky change
to a flaming panorama of gold and lavender and wild
rose and listen while Adam told her stories about the
place—sometimes Aboriginal legends, sometimes salty
yarns about the colourful eccentrics who were scattered
in the far-flung recesses of the area.

It was impossible in such circumstances for Caroline
to go on holding herself aloof. Each morning she had
to endure the torment of seeing Adam stripped naked,

rotating luxuriously under the brief downpour of the camp shower. Her first timid suggestion that he might leave his underwear on while doing this was met with such derision that she thought it more dignified not to argue. Thereafter she retired into the shelter each morning, but she could not help catching brief glimpses of him, which she found alarmingly provocative. He had a magnificent body, honed by hard work and outdoor life to an athletic power and grace that she had never imagined possible. His muscles rippled under his honey-gold skin when he raised his arms to wash his neck, and his taut waist tapered down to narrow hips and powerful, vigorous thighs. More than once Caroline caught herself staring wistfully at him, and her straying thoughts sent a jolt of shock through her. However much her reason might make her want to remain aloof, her body seemed to have its own ideas on the subject. To her shame, she soon found that she only needed to glance at him in order to have the most tantalisingly explicit pictures rioting through her head.

What was even worse, she was beginning to find herself emotionally drawn to Adam. Although he could be ruthless, he was often surprisingly considerate in an off-handed way. Whenever they were trekking over rugged country, he always carried the heaviest gear and unobtrusively lent her a hand in the hardest spots. And when it came to sharing the chores around the camp, he took the hardest jobs himself. More and more she found herself wondering why he had never married. With his blunt, forthright interrogation, Adam had extracted a good deal of information from Caroline about her own failed marriage, but he gave tantalisingly little in return. It went against her nature to pry, but one night she found herself asking him casually whether he had ever had any serious romantic involvement. For some reason, the answer seemed unbearably important, and she clenched her hands in her pockets and watched his frown deepen in the leaping firelight. 'Nobody special,' he replied with a brief grimace, and turned the conversation to the best method of roasting goannas. In the days that followed Caroline found herself pondering over this unsatis-factory reply and began to feel a powerful urge to break through Adam's iron-hard reserve.

Whether he suffered a similar torment in relation to her, she had no way of knowing, for his inscrutable face gave little away. Yet she was certain of one thing: the sexual attraction which had flared between them on their first meeting remained just as potent as ever. More than once Adam put an arm around her shoulders or bent to kiss the back of her neck when she was washing up, and each time a thrill of pure, molten longing coursed through her. Yet she successfully schooled herself into appearing indifferent, and it was not until almost the end of their trip that the spark between them was fanned into a runaway blaze.

Two weeks of uneventful bathing in the rock pool near the camp had almost extinguished Caroline's terror of crocodiles, but Adam still humoured her by sitting nearby with a rifle whenever she swam. And when danger finally appeared, it came from an unexpected source.

One morning she emerged dripping from the pool and groped for her towel. Turning her back on Adam, she dried her face and squeezed the water out of her hair, before briskly towelling her arms and chest. She was just stretching out one long, slim leg to begin drying it when Adam spoke in a hushed, warning undertone.

'Stay very still, Caroline. Whatever you do, don't step back. There's a snake right behind you.'

Terror reeled through her entire body and for one ghastly moment she was afraid she might faint and fall on the reptile anyway. But Adam's husky voice soothed her.

'You're all right, sweetheart. Just stay still, that's my brave girl. Don't move, I'm coming for you.'

Her ears strained for the sound of his approach, but she could hear nothing as he inched across the clearing.

Then there was a faint, ominous slithering movement in the dust behind her. Her heart gave a violent leap and her breath came in swift, terrified gulps. Desperately she forced herself to remain motionless, then to her relief she heard a soft footfall only metres away from her.

'All right, now put your right foot down in front of you and turn very slowly round to face me.'

With agonising slowness she obeyed. To her horror she saw Adam crouching in the dust with a snake coiled gracefully in his arms. It was about six feet long, brassy brown in colour, and its broad head was delicately pinched between his thumb and forefinger. With his free hand he was stroking the top of the head as he crooned softly to the reptile. The snake moved sinuously as if enjoying the caress and its tongue flickered in and out of its mouth. Caroline let out a ragged sigh of relief. Obviously Adam wouldn't be holding it like that if it were a really poisonous species, but it might still give him a nasty bite.

'Go and fetch me the thick sack from the back of the jeep and some twine to tie it with,' he whispered. 'Move past me very quietly, and don't run in case you startle it.'

Caroline forced her trembling legs to carry her past the glossy brown reptile. It seemed like hours until she came back with the sack and the length of twine.

'OK. Now hold the sack open as wide as you can while I lower him in,' instructed Adam. 'Don't worry, he can't bite, because I've got control of his head.'

Twice the snake rose up again like a jack-in-the-box, but at last Adam succeeded in thrusting its head well down and with a single, deft movement twisted the neck of the sack, snatched the twine and tied it firmly. Then he dropped the sack in the scrub.

'Phew!' he muttered. 'I'm glad that's over. I'll drive him out later and dump him somewhere in the bush well away from the camp. Are you all right? You look a bit pale.'

Caroline shuddered.

'I thought it was a poisonous one at first,' she admitted. 'And then I saw you handling it I realised it couldn't be. But it still scared the life out of me.'

Adam's lips twisted into a wry grin.

'I hate to disillusion you,' he said, 'but you really ought to know in case you meet another one of those. That was a taipan.'

'A taipan?' echoed Caroline in horror. 'But...but isn't that one of the most deadly snakes in the world?'

'That's right,' agreed Adam. 'You'd have been pretty sick if he'd bitten you. The poison affects the central nervous system and causes paralysis. In most cases death follows in a couple of hours, unless you can get to a hospital and have a shot of anti-venene.'

Caroline's senses reeled with shock.

'But you were holding it,' she croaked. 'Stroking it! Why?'

Adam absentmindedly plucked a piece of grass and chewed on the stem.

'I had to,' he said flatly. 'You were so close to it I couldn't risk shooting. I might have hit you or startled it into biting you.'

'But you could have been bitten yourself!' she cried wildly. 'How could you take such a risk? You might have died! And what would I have done then?'

'You'd have been all right,' he told her carelessly. 'There's plenty of food in the camp, and Danny Japulula would have come out in a couple of days and found you.'

'I didn't mean that!' shouted Caroline with an edge of hysteria in her voice. 'It's you I was thinking about... Paralysis... Oh, my God, you stupid, crazy, reckless——' Her self-control faltered and then vanished. She took a long, crowing breath and covered her face. 'You fool!' she wailed.

Adam flung away his grass stalk and moved towards her.

'Hey, hey, what's all this?' he demanded, drawing her into the comforting warmth of his arms. 'You're not crying, are you? It was nothing serious.'

With an incoherent mumble, she burrowed into his chest and gulped for breath. As her breasts brushed against the coarse cloth of his shirt, she realised belatedly that she was still naked. But it didn't seem to matter. Nothing seemed to matter except the fact that Adam could easily have been lying on the ground having convulsions and losing consciousness, while she stood despairingly by and watched him die. Instead he was here, safe, strong and full of vitality, crushing her against him. She put her arms around his waist and squeezed him hard.

'I'm so glad you didn't die!' she babbled, raising her face to his. 'I couldn't bear if it you'd died!'

He smiled wryly.

'I'm glad to hear it,' he said. 'Now come on back to the fire and I'll make you some coffee. It'll help you get over the shock.'

But when he tried to disengage himself from her, she clung instinctively to the lapels of his shirt. 'Wait,' she begged.

He paused, scanning her features with a concerned expression.

'I'm sorry,' she muttered huskily. 'I'll be all right now.'

With a long, shuddering sigh, she released her hold on his shirt and smiled tremulously at him. Then she leant forward and tried to pick up her towel, but her hands were shaking so much that she dropped it. Adam made an impatient noise and scooped her up in his arms.

'You're suffering from shock,' he muttered. 'You'd better come and lie down.'

Caroline snuggled dizzily into his shoulder and closed her eyes as he strode impatiently across the clearing. Her senses were still in turmoil from the encounter with the taipan, but she had never in her life known such a sense of safety as she felt now in Adam's arms. His body was warm and hard against hers and she felt herself relaxing against him. She felt frail, protected, feminine, and found the experience surprisingly alluring. A fierce primeval impulse swept through her that made her want to surrender totally to him and glory in her submission. Scarcely aware of what she was doing, she nestled more closely into his grip so that the warm curve of her breast brushed against his hand. His body stiffened, but he kept walking steadily until they reached the shelter. Crouching down, he held back the tarpaulin flap and carried her inside. Then he dropped her unceremoniously on the bed.

'I'll make some coffee,' he said curtly.

'Wait,' she begged. 'Don't leave me, Adam.'

Her eyes were dark with longing as she stretched out her hands to him. With a muffled groan he sat down on the bed and stared unwaveringly at her.

'You know, I can't figure out whether you're incredibly innocent or incredibly devious,' he growled.

'W-what are you talking about?' faltered Caroline.

Adam swore softly.

'I'm talking about this,' he hissed.

And, seizing her hand, he guided it down to the waistband of his shorts and pressed it fiercely against him. Caroline gave a low gasp of shock as she felt his swollen male hardness through the coarse fabric. Then, lying down beside her, he whispered in her ear and gave her an even worse shock.

'Don't you realise that you're asking for trouble?' he demanded in a harsh, pitiless undertone. 'Don't you have the slightest understanding of your own desires or mine? If I stay in this tent now, I intend to kiss every inch of your body slowly and then order you to undress me and do the same to me. And after that I'm going to make love to you until you explode with passion and whimper and writhe about and beg me to stop. But I won't stop. Because if I'm going to have you at all, Caroline Faircroft, I'm going to have you until I'm completely sated with you. Now do you understand?'

A mysterious throbbing began to pulse through her entire body, sending wave after wave of delicious heat through her limbs. She felt vaguely that his words were outrageous, and yet they sparked off a wild, irrational yearning that threatened to blaze up and consume her.

'Well?' insisted Adam. 'Do you understand?'

Caroline felt a small, catlike smile curving on her lips. Her tongue touched the back of her teeth.

'Yes,' she admitted huskily.

'And do you want me to go?'

She wanted to say 'yes' again, but somehow her lips refused to frame the word. Adam's face was so close that she could see the gold stubble on his chin and feel his shallow, rapid breathing against her neck. Hesitantly she reached out and trailed her fingers down his cheek, bringing them to rest on the powerful angle of his jaw.

'No,' she said hoarsely.

He caught his breath and then hauled her against him. For an instant he loomed above her, lean and tanned and hungry-looking, while one of his hands played idly with her unruly brown hair.

'Oh, Caroline,' he murmured throatily. 'You little witch!'

Then his mouth came down on hers. Caroline had never imagined that mere kissing could be so wildly erotic. At first Adam's kisses were only teasing encounters, butterfly-soft tremors that fluttered over her lips and throat and shoulders, making her quiver and giggle. But then they deepened and grew slower, more penetrating, more demanding. Soon her mouth was opening eagerly to his and his merciless, tormenting hands were sending spirals of flame shooting through her entire body. His thumb traced a lazy whorl over the tender flesh of her nipple, making it harden into a tight, aroused nub. A low moan escaped her and she arched her back, pressing herself against him until he smiled slyly and bent his head to her other breast. Shudders of excitement coursed through her at the tingling caress of his tongue, but her response only goaded him to greater efforts.

'You taste delicious,' he murmured. 'Like wild honey. I could eat you up, do you know that?'

His mouth was so close to her flesh that she could feel the tickling warmth of his breath on her skin. Deliberately he nuzzled her midriff, making a soft growling sound in the back of his throat as if he were a bear eating her up. She wriggled delightedly, unable to suppress a gasp of laughter as his stubbly chin scraped her flesh. But even that prickly touch was unexpectedly sensual, sending currents of electricity tingling through her.

'Why are you laughing?' he asked lazily.

'You're tickling me.'

'Do you want me to stop?'

'No. It feels like . . . Oh, Adam!'

For in a sudden swoop his lips had moved lower still and he was teasing her with slow, sensual motions of his tongue in a way that she had never dreamt possible. She gasped and tried to struggle up, but he pushed her ruthlessly back against the pillow.

'Adam, you can't . . . ,' she protested weakly.

His glance took in her wildly dilated eyes, the flush that was rising on her cheeks, the way her breath came and went in shallow gulps. And a slow, triumphant smile spread over his face. In that instant he looked every inch the predatory male, powerful, ruthless and arrogantly certain of his own virility.

'Oh, can't I?' he murmured. 'Well, I'm damned if I'm going to stop now, sweetheart, so why don't you just close your eyes and enjoy it?'

She gave a brief, protesting whimper, which changed into a low, sensual moan as Adam's lips went back to work. Without any conscious intention on her part her eyelids fluttered shut and she felt herself floating into an ecstatic whirlwind of pleasure. Dimly she realised that Adam was only doing this for his own satisfaction. She knew perfectly well that he didn't love her, and yet it no longer seemed to matter. Nothing seemed to matter except the exquisite, tormenting, violent compulsion of need that was sending her thrusting and whimpering against his questing mouth. Time lost all meaning as her fingers tightened in his thick blond hair and she pulled him urgently against her. Her tension spiralled until suddenly a dark heat seemed to explode inside her, setting off a series of convulsive, quivering movements that made her whole body clench uncontrollably.

'Oh. Oh. Oh,' she cried. 'Oh, Adam!'

For a long, long moment ecstasy held her in its grip, then she fell back to earth. Her eyelids fluttered open. The dark outlines of the shelter rushed dizzily at her and she lay, feeling disorientated and strange, listening to the hammering of her own blood in her ears and hearing herself gulping for breath. In a moment the world reorganised itself around her and she looked up with wildly dilated eyes to see Adam kneeling over her naked body. His face was contorted with passion and there was a triumphant gleam in his eyes.

'I always knew you'd be passionate, Caroline,' he murmured. 'But I didn't expect fireworks quite like that. Well, now it's my turn.'

Seizing her slim white hands, he planted a kiss inside each palm and then carried them to the top button of his shirt.

'Undress me,' he commanded.

A shudder went through her that might have been fear or passion or reluctance. Or perhaps all three. But this new, strange Caroline who seemed to have taken over her body did not draw back. With tantalising slowness her long, slender fingers unfastened the buttons of his shirt. And all the time she was working, she held him captive with her eyes. When at last the shirt was open, revealing the hard, tanned muscles of Adam's chest, she slipped her hands inside it. For a moment she closed her eyes, revelling in the touch of his skin that was as slick as oiled silk. Then her fingers slid up to caress the rough mat of hair that grew there. Hesitantly she traced lingering circles, then let her hands wander round to his back, where they trickled shyly up and down his spine. A shudder went through him, and she felt a heady sense of excitement at the realisation of her own power. Was it really possible that she could send Adam plunging into the same breathless, heady rapture that he gave to her? Her eyes met his with a sly, smouldering question and his hand came out and smoothed back her hair, then touched the side of her mouth in a brief caress.

'You're irresistible,' he murmured hoarsely.

She smiled secretively and turned her mouth to meet his hand. Biting softly on his thumb, she closed her lips on it and sucked it with long, slow strokes. Adam groaned softly.

'Too much more of this and I'll just go quietly insane,' he muttered. 'All right, you shameless little witch. Nothing's going to save you now.'

He was still kneeling astride her, but now he seized her by the shoulders and hauled her roughly into a sitting position. Then he guided her fingers to the buckle of his belt.

'Go on,' he ordered.

She should have been horrified, but if she was shaking it was from eagerness, not fear. Her fingers fumbled urgently on the buckle, then, with a fierce tug, she tore it free. Sliding her hands inside his shorts, she peeled them slowly down, then caught her breath and looked at him.

'Oh, Adam,' she breathed.

He rose to his feet and stood for a moment, proud and naked and heartachingly virile, then he kicked away the shorts and came to her.

'Oh, hell, I want you, Caroline,' he said in a tense, throbbing voice. 'You can't imagine how much I want you.'

Twining his fingers in her tumbled brown hair, he drew her against him and kissed her fiercely. Stars exploded behind her eyes and she yielded to the dark, instinctive urge to burrow blindly into his embrace. His nearness sent shudders of longing coursing through her, and when he took her hand and urged her to touch him more intimately she obeyed with a readiness that stunned her. It was as if her whole life had been moving towards this moment. The moment when fear would fall away from her and she would be fully a woman, proud, joyful and free to love.

'Kiss me, Caroline,' urged Adam. 'I want to feel you driving me wild, just the way I did to you.'

For a moment she hesitated, feeling her breath coming in long, agonising gasps, as if she had been running. But only for a moment. Then, like some jungle creature, she drew herself up proudly and swung one long, slim leg across his body. Swooping forward, she let her hair fall in a swinging cascade that tickled his face. Then she stretched herself out slowly and deliberately and lay down full length on top of him.

'Mmmm,' murmured Adam hoarsely. 'Wonderful.'

Caroline gave a soft giggle at this frank sensuality, and suddenly the last of her anxiety vanished. A spreading warmth invaded her entire body and was followed by a sense of glorious, transcendent joy. You are magnificent, Adam, she thought fiercely. You've really shown me how incredibly satisfying passion can be. And with an impulsive urge to return the pleasure he had given her, she wriggled sensually down his body, letting her breasts brush tantalisingly against him. Adam groaned ecstatically and seizing her by the hair, thrust her fiercely downwards.

Soon there was no sound in the shelter but their inarticulate cries and rapid, shallow breathing. But at last Adam could bear it no longer. Gripping her fiercely in his arms, he rolled wildly with her until he was lying on top of her, pinioning her beneath him.

'Are you ready?' he demanded hoarsely.

'Yes. Yes. Oh, yes,' she panted.

The touch of his warm, male hardness made her gasp with longing. She gazed up into his face and saw that his blue eyes looked dark and strange with desire. And then like a flashback from a nightmare his rugged features were briefly blotted out. In his place she saw Jeremy, angry, half drunk and determined to humiliate her. Her entire body stiffened and she caught her breath. Then the moment passed and she was gazing once more at Adam. But Adam too had changed. He was no longer staring down at her with smouldering passion in his eyes. Instead his face was grim with suspicion and resentment.

'What is it?' he demanded. 'What's wrong?' And then, in a slow, incredulous snarl, 'Were you thinking of Jeremy?'

Her face set into a frozen mask of horror. She stared at him mutely, knowing that her lips were moving, but unable to utter a sound. He caught her by the shoulders and shook her violently.

'Well, were you?' he insisted savagely. 'Answer me!'

Her eyes were wide with shock and dismay. She tried to speak, but could only make a strangled whimper in the back of her throat. She wanted to say that she hated Jeremy and that the memories terrified and disgusted her, but the words wouldn't come.

'Answer me, damn you!' thundered Adam. 'Were you thinking of Jeremy?'

'Yes,' she choked.

Adam swore violently and rose to his feet. Then, picking up a pile of her clothes that lay neatly folded on a camp chair, he flung them at her.

'Get dressed!' he ordered savagely. 'We're going back home.'

CHAPTER FIVE

FOR the second time Caroline and Adam travelled back to Winnamurra Station amid an atmosphere that crackled with tension. The camp had been dismantled with a speed and energy that bordered on frenzy, and all their equipment was thrown helter-skelter into the back of the jeep. What was worse, Adam vented all his rage on his driving, sending the vehicle hurtling over jagged escarpments and down boulder-strewn slopes in a way that made Caroline fear for her life. Now and then, when she wasn't being jolted violently against the windscreen or clinging apprehensively to her seat, she tried to make sense of what had happened between them. To her dismay, she realised that her chief reaction was not relief at Adam's abrupt ending of their encounter. It was disappointment.

She wished she could explain to him. Yet how could she endure the humiliation of telling him the truth? Of admitting that Jeremy had totally destroyed her confidence in her ability to form another relationship? Of telling him that the mere memory of her ex-husband was enough to turn her to stone in another man's arms? After all, hadn't Jeremy told her again and again that she was unresponsive and incapable of giving or receiving pleasure in lovemaking? Well, some of her long-held doubts were now beginning to crumble. Jeremy had been wrong about one thing, at least, she thought defiantly. She knew now that she could experience a passion that made her gasp with its intensity. But what if events had proceeded to their natural conclusion? Wouldn't Adam have found her a terrible disappointment as a partner? For an agonised moment she toyed with the thought of sharing these fears with him, but a single glance at his

face made her dismiss the idea. His face was set in a
murderous scowl and he sat hunched forward over the
wheel, his knuckles showing white through his tan. With
a growing sense of dread, Caroline realised that there
was an almighty confrontation brewing.

Yet when they reached the dusty red stockyards and
one of the cattlemen hailed them loudly, Adam stopped
the vehicle and climbed out with a smile on his face and
a civil greeting on his lips. A few moments were spent
answering questions and giving orders, then he climbed
back in beside Caroline and drove her up to the house.
Slamming the door, he came around to her side of the
jeep and stood with his hands on his hips as she climbed
out. She saw then quite clearly that his pleasant manner
was reserved for other people. His eyes were smoky with
contempt as he gazed at her and a pulse was beating an
angry tattoo in his throat.

'Go inside and get showered and changed,' he ordered
brusquely. 'I've got work to do and I don't have time
to deal with you now. But I'll see you in my office at
nine o'clock tomorrow morning. There are things we
need to discuss.'

Caroline's throat ached with unshed tears as she
watched him stride swiftly across to one of the machinery sheds without a backward glance. She could
hardly have felt more humiliated if he had slapped her
face. Every nuance of his speech, every movement of
his body proclaimed the same message: I am the boss
here and you will do exactly as I say. If a chasm could
have opened beneath her feet and hidden her from Adam
Fletcher forever, Caroline would have jumped gladly into
it. As it was, she was completely trapped and had no
option but to obey him. Dragging her feet, she walked
slowly up the stairs and inside the house.

Some impulse of rebellion made her refuse to take a
shower immediately, but, after she had sat in the kitchen
for ten minutes sipping orange juice, she realised how
ridiculous she was being. All right, Adam Fletcher was

an arrogant swine, but there was no point defying him over trivial matters. Much better to save her ammunition for something important. Like the fire lilies? she wondered, as she padded down the hall towards her bathroom. The thought made her stop dead in her tracks. She knew she had wounded Adam profoundly, but surely he wouldn't be vindictive enough to prevent her obtaining the plants? Or would he? Wasn't it entirely likely that he would ask her to leave Winnamurra?

Once inside the bathroom, she stripped off her dirty clothes and climbed thankfully into the shower. For five minutes, a welcome oblivion descended on her as the water sluiced away all the grime of the expedition. But when she had finished shampooing her hair and scrubbing her skin, her brain reluctantly came to life again. Turning off the taps, she climbed out of the shower and began listlessly drying herself. In spite of her resolve not to let Adam upset her, an overpowering sense of misery seemed to be welling up inside her. After pulling on blue and white shorts and a matching top, she cleared a little window in the steam on the mirror so that she could comb her hair. But instead she simply sat there staring into her own unhappy grey eyes. Then with an impatient sigh she rested her chin on her clenched fist.

'I don't have to leave,' she explained to her reflection. 'I just don't want to leave. If I have to go, I'll miss him dreadfully.'

The thought appalled her. Here she was, twenty-eight years old, divorced, independent and with a successful career, yet turning to mush like some lovesick teenager. Could Caroline Faircroft, cool, poised, efficient botanist, really be acting like this?

'Well, it's not actually Adam that I'll miss,' she tried to assure herself. 'It's just that I'll feel so badly about giving up the fire lily project.'

Her reflection smiled sceptically back at her with a faint lift of the eyebrows.

'Oh, who do I think I'm kidding?' she wailed. 'Of course I'd be sorry to give up the fire lilies, but it's Adam I really want.'

That realisation sent her into a tailspin of panic, as she tried to examine her feelings. All right, so she wanted Adam. But what exactly did she want from him? Walking into the bedroom, she paced restlessly around, rubbing her damp hair and trying to calm her seething emotions. There could be no real doubt any more that she wanted him physically. Her body seemed to quiver and throb in the most extraordinary manner at the mere touch of his hands or the sound of his voice, but was it just a meaningless sexual current, or did she genuinely care about him? To put it bluntly, was she in love with him? Yet the mere thought of that made her shy away. Her only experience of falling in love so far had been so brutally disillusioning that the words no longer meant anything to her. All she knew was that Adam Fletcher seemed to touch something deep inside her. For the first time since her divorce she felt as if she might want to risk the pain of involvement again. In fact it might even be wonderfully exciting to get to know Adam better, to spend time in the slow, intimate unfolding of friendship and trust...

Except that she was hardly likely to have a chance to do anything of the sort, she reminded herself. Adam's words rang ominously in her ears. 'There are things we need to discuss.' It didn't take much imagination to work out what the discussion was likely to cover!

In spite of her resolutions to be poised and nonchalant, Caroline felt her heart beating in a wild, uneven rhythm when she tapped on the office door the following morning.

'Come in.'

Adam's voice was unmistakably surly.

'Good morning,' fluttered Caroline uncertainly.

There was no response, apart from an impatient shrug. She advanced warily, holding her folder of botanical notes in front of her like a protective shield. Then she lowered herself into a chair. Adam leaned forward across his desk and fixed her with a cool, appraising stare. Unnerved by his gaze, she spoke.

'I expect you want me to leave,' she faltered.

Why did I say that? she wondered despairingly. Now I've given him exactly the opening he wants! Yet Adam did not rush to reply. Instead he sat surveying her through narrowed blue eyes with an enigmatic smile hovering around the corners of his lips. The silence lengthened agonisingly.

'No,' he said at last. 'I think that would be a ridiculous overreaction to a very trivial incident.'

Trivial! Caroline flushed deeply at this casual dismissal of the encounter. To her it had been fraught with meaning, and yet Adam could sit here calmly telling her it was trivial! Her hands twisted in her lap and she felt her fingernails dig into her palms. Then she clutched at her folder and sat up rigidly erect.

'I suppose that's true,' she said, tossing her head. 'So it's all right for me to stay, is it?'

'I didn't say that.' Adam's tone was cool, measured, indifferent.

She stared at him in perplexity. 'But if you don't want me to go and you don't want me to stay——' she began.

He held up one hand in a gesture of command.

'It doesn't really matter to me what you do,' he said. 'But I don't want to keep enticing you into these meaningless encounters. In some ways it might be best if you did go, but you've convinced me that this fire lily project is worthwhile. So I've only one thing to suggest.'

'What's that?' she asked uneasily.

'That you and I go away together for a while.'

Caroline caught her breath. The words 'meaningless encounters' stung her like a whiplash, but she was determined not to let Adam see her distress. If he could be so maddeningly calm and uncaring, then so could she!

'Oh, you're planning another little trip into the bush, are you?' she demanded sarcastically.

'No, I'm not!' he retorted. 'Because let me tell you, sweetheart, I have absolutely no ambition to make love to you while you close your eyes and pretend I'm your precious ex-husband! What I'm suggesting is that we should go to Canberra for a week or so.'

'Canberra?' she echoed in a baffled voice.

'Yes, Canberra. The nation's capital. You have heard of it, presumably?'

'Of course I've heard of it!' she snapped. 'But why on earth should we go there? It must be two thousand miles away.'

'I'll tell you why,' said Adam, folding his arms and scowling at her. 'Canberra has one big advantage that Winnamurra Station doesn't. Once we're there, we can keep well away from each other. Or do you think you'd prefer to be cooped up in this place together for the next week?'

Caroline's head filled with sudden images of what might happen and she blushed a dull red.

'Exactly,' drawled Adam insultingly. 'I think we might be safer in Canberra out of temptation's way, don't you?'

'But why Canberra?' she persisted.

'I have to go down there this month on business anyway, so I'll just bring the trip forward by a week or two.'

'Oh, what sort of business?' she asked.

'I need to have a little chat with the Minister for Primary Industry about our trade deficit,' replied Adam in a deadpan voice.

For a moment Caroline's eyes widened. Then she gave a groan of reluctant laughter. 'Pull the other leg,' she advised. 'What are you really going there for?'

He surveyed her out of narrowed blue eyes.

'No, the Minister wouldn't really want to talk to a back-country cowboy like me, would he?' he drawled acidly. 'Well, let's just say that I want to see some of my old friends from my days in the public service. Now are you coming with me or not?'

Caroline hesitated.

'Do I have a choice?' she asked.

'Sure. You can go back to England if you prefer. But if you still want to collect those fire lilies, you'll stay where I can keep an eye on you.'

His mouth was set in such a grim line that she gave in.

'All right,' she agreed. 'But how do we get there? It's too far to drive, isn't it?'

'We'll fly,' replied Adam. 'I have a light aircraft that I use on the property. We can take that to Alice Springs and then catch a commercial flight to Canberra.'

'You mean you're a qualified pilot?' she demanded.

'Yes, but don't look so startled. It's nearly as common as having a driver's licence in these parts.'

Yet Caroline was startled. A vivid image of Adam riding on camel-back flashed before her, and she realised that she had always thought of him as some kind of wild nomad. It was an image that the last two weeks had done little to dispel. Now she began to wonder whether there was more to him than she had ever suspected.

She wondered even more strongly the following morning in Alice Springs when they met in the lobby of their hotel to take a taxi to the airport. Instead of the old army shorts, battered Akubra hat and elastic-sided boots which were his usual garb, Adam was impeccably dressed in a charcoal-grey suit, white shirt and pale blue and grey tie. His black shoes gleamed, his face was smoothly shaven and he carried an expensive briefcase in his right hand. Slung carelessly over his left arm was a stylish Italian overcoat. Caroline gaped at him.

'I can't believe it's you!' she said.

He smiled thinly.

'Well, I wouldn't want to embarrass you in Canberra,' he murmured. 'Especially when you look so charming yourself.'

Caroline stared at him suspiciously, uncertain whether she was being mocked. She was wearing the one and only good dress she had brought with her, the floral print in tones of deep blue and rust, but she definitely didn't feel that she matched up to Adam.

'Won't you boil in those clothes?' she asked hesitantly. 'It must be thirty-five degrees centigrade outside.'

Adam's white teeth flashed in amusement.

'It's hot up here in the tropics, but it won't be in Canberra,' he reminded her. 'It's midwinter right now, or had you forgotten?'

She stared at him in consternation.

'Yes, I had,' she admitted. 'I haven't even got a coat with me.'

'Don't worry. I'll buy you one when we get there,' he said.

She opened her mouth to protest, then paused. The cost of a decent winter coat would make an alarming hole in her diminishing resources.

'I—I can't possibly let you,' she stammered.

'You'll have to,' replied Adam suavely. 'I don't want you freezing to death. And you'd better get a long evening dress while you're at it. I'm taking you to a dinner with a few of my friends tomorrow night.'

Just at that moment their taxi arrived, so Caroline had little opportunity to argue. But once they were aboard the plane, she puzzled over the conversation. Why on earth would she need a long evening dress to attend a dinner with Adam's friends? Wouldn't they just be other cattlemen on holiday or minor public servants? The sort of people who would gather for a friendly steak and chips washed down by a beer in the local pub? So why would she need a long dress for that? She darted a puzzled glance at Adam and was answered with a sardonic lift of his eyebrow. An uneasy suspicion began to grow in her that he was setting her up for some kind of practical joke.

The suspicion hardened into certainty when they were met at the Canberra airport by a chauffeur in a grey government uniform.

'Good morning, Mr Fletcher,' he said, touching his cap. 'Good to see you again, sir.'

Adam gave him a warm smile.

'Nice to see you too, Alf,' he said. 'Alf's an old mate of mine, Caroline. We worked in the same department years ago. Alf, this is Dr Caroline Faircroft from the Morrow Museum in London.'

'How do you do, ma'am?' said the chauffeur formally.

Caroline's eyes widened in disbelief. How on earth had Adam organised this? she wondered. Poor old Alf would probably lose his job if anyone found out he was driving his friends around in government cars! All the same, it was a rather splendid joke.

'Hello, Alf,' she murmured in a voice full of barely suppressed laughter.

Alf set their luggage on a trolley, then led them out of the building to a gleaming black limousine.

'Now where to, sir?' he asked, when he had finished stowing their bags.

'A quick tour around the city sights,' ordered Adam. 'And then take us to the shopping mall in the city centre. Dr Faircroft needs some winter clothes. After that you can take us home.'

As the car headed away from the airport, Caroline looked eagerly out of the window. Adam had been right about the weather. In her brief passage from the heated arrivals lounge to the car, she had been met by a blast of chill, invigorating air. Yet in spite of this the sun was shining brightly and the city had a look of newly washed brilliance about it. Much of the native forest had been left untouched and the streets were bordered by strips of lawn planted with European trees, so that it was rather like driving through a vast garden. Alf proudly pointed out the huge new Parliament House building, the War Memorial, Lake Burley Griffin and other landmarks, and then, as they neared the city centre, his pretence of honouring a visiting dignitary flagged a little.

'What do you reckon about Hawthorn beating Collingwood in next Saturday's game, mate?' he asked. 'I've got ten dollars that says Hawthorn will win.'

'Have you?' jeered Adam. 'Well, in my opinion, they haven't got a hope. Besides, I wouldn't have the heart to take your money, Alf.'

'Aargh! Too flaming smart to risk losing your own brass, cobber. That's the truth,' replied Alf genially. 'Now, is this where you want to go?'

He parked the car and settled himself comfortably with a newspaper while Adam ushered Caroline into a shopping mall. Once inside the building, he paused to look at a directory of the shops. Caroline put her hand on his arm.

'Adam, Alf won't get into trouble for this, will he?' she asked earnestly.

He glanced down at her sharply.

'What do you mean?' he demanded.

'Well, that's a genuine government limousine outside, isn't it?'

'Yes,' said Adam in a wondering tone.

'And Alf is a genuine chauffeur, isn't he?'

'Yes,' he agreed again.

'Look,' continued Caroline, 'I think it was a brilliant joke to have him meet us at the airport as if you really were some kind of visiting dignitary instead of just an old friend of his. But won't he get into trouble for it?'

Adam bit his lip as if he were trying not to laugh.

'You never for an instant believed that I was a genuine visiting dignitary?' he challenged.

'Well, of course not!' she retorted. 'I'm not that stupid! Besides, you wouldn't be making bets with your driver about football games if you were, would you?'

He stared at her with an unreadable expression.

'This is Australia,' he reminded her, 'and Aussies don't stand on ceremony much. But your instincts are sound,

Caroline. I'm really much more of a cowboy at heart than a stuffed-shirt civil servant. Now let's go and buy that coat.'

With a vague feeling of uneasiness, she allowed him to steer her into a small boutique that had a window full of elegant men's and women's clothing. An exquisitely groomed blonde woman with a ravishing smile and a rather predatory expression came gliding across to meet them. Adam drawled an explanation and Caroline was led away and left to examine a rack of beautiful evening dresses. They looked very attractive, but when Caroline fumbled through them she was alarmed to find that there were no price tags on any of them. An old saying popped into her head; 'If you need to ask the price, you can't afford it.' Adam was sitting on a Chippendale chair, looking as casual and relaxed as if he were by an outback waterhole, and she beckoned frantically to him.

'What is it?' he asked, lounging across to her with a slight frown. 'Don't you like any of them?'

'It's not that. I don't think I can afford them,' she hissed.

His brow cleared.

'You don't need to,' he said bluntly. 'I already told you, I'm paying for this. Now, how about this one?'

He held up a V-necked blue taffeta dress with a corded bodice and butterfly sleeves. Caroline looked longingly at it. The colour would suit her perfectly.

'Go on,' urged Adam. 'I don't want to keep Alf waiting too long.'

This brusque reminder had the desired effect. Instead of arguing, Caroline took the dress and vanished into a changing cubicle. When she emerged a couple of minutes later, Adam was leaning on the counter chatting to the saleswoman. He paused in mid-sentence and let his gaze travel critically down over Caroline's slender form.

'Not bad,' he said. 'We'll take that one, thanks. And how about that tan woollen coat on the dummy in the window?'

'But——' Caroline began.

'Come on,' prompted Adam, looking at his watch. 'I haven't got all day, you know.'

With a rapturous sigh at this masterful behaviour, the saleswoman rushed to wrestle the coat off the dummy.

'Oh, what's the use?' muttered Caroline and, taking the garment, disappeared once more into the cubicle.

Fifteen minutes later they emerged into the car park, laden with bags. Caroline had two, containing her dress and coat, and Adam must have done some shopping on his account, for he was carrying another three.

'Right. Home, please, Alf,' he ordered, handing Caroline into the back seat of the car.

'What do you mean by "home"?' she whispered, as the car purred away. 'You don't have a house here, do you?'

'Yes, I do, as a matter of fact,' replied Adam carelessly. 'I used to live in Canberra from time to time, and after I left my job a couple of years ago I decided to keep the place to use when I'm in town. Besides, it's a good investment.'

'But aren't you afraid people might burgle it while you're not here?' she asked.

'Good question,' he admitted. 'But an old friend who I was at school with works in Canberra a lot and he stays in it when he's here. His name's Mark Sloane. Nice chap. He'll be at the dinner tomorrow night.'

The house proved to be a surprisingly attractive two-storey building, set in half an acre of grounds, flanked on either side by foreign ambassadors' residences. Caroline's eyes widened as Adam led her into a wood-panelled hall, dominated by a huge gilt mirror and an antique hall cupboard adorned with two huge Ming vases.

'This is absolutely beautiful!' she exclaimed in amazement.

He shrugged.

'I suppose so,' he admitted. 'Houses bore me really, but I needed this one to look good for my job, so I let the decorators have their heads.'

'What kind of job were you doing exactly?' asked Caroline.

'One where I entertained a lot,' he replied curtly. 'And speaking of jobs, I must get to work. I've got a meeting at four o'clock and a business dinner at eight, so I'm not likely to be home before midnight. Can you fend for yourself if I leave you here?'

'Yes, I suppose so,' she began. 'But what——?'

'I've got to go,' Adam cut in. 'Oh, by the way, I bought you a few more clothes that you might find useful. Here, catch!'

He flung the three carrier-bags at her in rapid succession like frisbees and a cascade of stylish sweaters, jackets, trousers, blouses and woollen skirts spilt all over the parquet floor. Caroline fell to her knees beside them with an appalled expression.

'I can't possibly afford all these!' she wailed. 'Why did you buy them without telling me? You must have known I'd refuse to accept them.'

Adam's white teeth parted in a knowing smile.

'That's exactly why I did it,' he explained. 'And in case you're thinking of going back for a refund, don't bother. They'll exchange them if you don't like them, but they have a policy of no refunds. See you later, sweetheart.'

Before she could protest, he was out the door, closing it behind him with a vigorous slam. Caroline let out her breath in a long, perplexed sigh, then picked up the scattered clothes and made her way into the drawing-room. This was a long, sunny room furnished with deep leather couches, carved Chinese tables, chunky lamps with oriental bases and a lot of feathery green pot plants. Sinking into a luxurious sofa, Caroline dropped the clothes and ran her fingers distractedly through her hair.

'I can't figure out what's going on here,' she complained aloud. 'What on earth is Adam Fletcher doing in a place like this?'

She had always assumed that Adam was a wild cowboy frontiersman more at home with a rifle than a book. Yet this house with its antiques and works of art, its laden bookshelves and expensive furniture, looked like the home of an educated, cultured man. Adam? No, it was impossible! These trappings must belong to his friend Mark Sloane. If Adam had ever read anything more difficult than a cereal packet, Caroline would eat her hat!

Giving up the puzzle with a shrug, she decided to explore the house. In addition to the drawing-room, the ground floor proved to have a lavishly equipped kitchen, a formal dining-room to seat twelve people, a study with computer terminals and a fax machine and a large bathroom complete with Jacuzzi. Upstairs there were two more bathrooms and five bedrooms. One of these showed signs of recent occupation, with folders scattered on a desk, a man's jacket flung carelessly over a chair and a family photo on a chest of drawers. Another held riding boots, an Akubra hat and a stockwhip, which clearly revealed it as Adam's territory, but the third one was unoccupied, so Caroline took it over.

Worn out by the trip from Alice Springs, she fixed herself an early supper of scrambled eggs and salad, looked through some brochures about Canberra which she found in the living-room, and then went to bed. She was woken shortly after one a.m. by the purr of Alf's limousine in the driveway and an hour later another set of headlights flashed across her ceiling. Yawning, Caroline turned over. Whatever work Adam and his friend did, they certainly kept late hours.

Yet when she came down to the kitchen at eight o'clock the following morning, she found Adam sitting at the table already shaved and dressed. He was reading a financial newspaper, but he glanced up as she slipped into a chair.

'You look nice,' he said in a neutral voice.

Caroline coloured delicately. She was wearing one of the outfits he had bought for her the day before—a silk blouse with a blue pleated skirt and a Fair Isle cardigan in blue and rust wool. Accepting gifts from him made her feel decidedly uncomfortable, but she knew when she was outmanoeuvred. Much as she hated giving in, it was really her only option.

Her thoughts must have shown in her face, for Adam gave her a mocking smile as he passed the coffee to her.

'So you're a sensible woman who bows to superior judgement, are you?' he asked.

She choked back the retort that rose to her lips and concentrated on pouring her coffee.

'Not going to bite?' he asked lazily. 'What a pity. Well, what plans do you have for today, may I ask? Sightseeing, shopping?'

Caroline shook her head.

'I'd really like to get in touch with some other botanists, if I could,' she said. 'But I'm not sure how to go about it. Perhaps I should phone the university.'

Adam nodded and delved in his pocket for a piece of paper. Smoothing it out, he passed it across to her.

'I had a feeling you might say that,' he remarked. 'That's the name and phone number of an old friend of mine, Patrick Edmundson. He's Professor of Australian Botany at the Australian National University. He should be able to help you.'

Caroline stared at him with a puzzled frown. How on earth would he know somebody like that?

'Thank you,' she murmured.

Adam looked amused.

'And now you're asking yourself how a wild outback cowboy like me knows a botany professor, aren't you?' he demanded shrewdly. 'Well, I'll put you out of your misery. We lived in the same college in our university days, although we took different degrees.'

Caroline blinked. Instead of satisfying her curiosity, Adam was simply raising a whole host of new questions in her mind. It had never even occurred to her that he might have studied at university. So what other unsuspected dimensions did he have?

He gave a wry chuckle at her obvious perplexity.

'I'm a man of many talents, Caroline,' he murmured in a deliberately mysterious voice. 'Roping steers and mending fences are only two of them. I'm also remarkably skilful at dialling telephone numbers, so if you'll just give me back that piece of paper I'll ring Pat and see if I can arrange a meeting for you.'

Two minutes later Adam set down the telephone receiver and gave her a brisk nod.

'Nine-thirty at the botany department,' he said. 'Finish your breakfast and I'll drive you over there.'

'There's no need——' began Caroline, but he cut her off.

'Pat can only spare you an hour,' he continued. 'And I'm not very busy today, so I'll pick you up again at ten-thirty and show you around the city.'

Then, without waiting for her reply, he buried himself in the financial paper again. Caroline could only stare at him in bewilderment. Even at Winnamurra Station, Adam had seemed a man born to command, but in Canberra that air of authority was subtly enhanced. In his elegant dark suit and crisp shirt, he gave off an aura of power that was completely unmistakable. Perhaps that was why she gave in to his suggestion without another whisper of protest.

When she emerged from Pat Edmundson's study, at ten-thirty, Adam was drinking coffee in the outer office where the secretary reigned. But the moment he saw Caroline he rose to his feet. Murmuring something that made the secretary smile and blush, he crossed the room to greet Caroline.

'How did it go?' he asked.

Her face glowed.

'It was super!' she cried, bubbling over. 'Professor Edmundson knows so much about the botany of the area, and all the customs regulations too. He's been tremendously helpful. And he's really excited about the fire lily project. Thank you so much for introducing me to him!'

Adam smiled at her enthusiasm.

'My pleasure,' he said.

Caroline paused to say goodbye to the secretary, then stood beaming as Adam helped her into her coat. But the moment they were outside, her joy bubbled over and she did a little dance on the pathway. Then she swung herself ecstatically in a circle round the trunk of a silver birch tree, while Adam stood watching her and shaking his head.

'Sorry,' she muttered penitently as she came bouncing back on to the other path. 'I'll come down to earth in a moment.'

'Don't!' he urged in an odd voice. 'You're rather enchanting when you're walking on air.'

Caroline stopped dead and stared at him. For a moment she thought he was mocking her, and then she decided that he wasn't. Her heart lurched painfully as she saw the warmth in his blue eyes. It was disconcerting, to say the least. After all, hadn't he called their passionate encounter in the bush 'a trivial incident' and then treated her as if he despised her? Then why was he looking at her now so intently? She caught her breath.

'What is it?' he demanded.

'I never know where I am with you,' she complained. 'I thought you hated me.'

He shrugged.

'I thought I did too,' he agreed. 'But perhaps we were both wrong. Anyway, where would you like to start your sightseeing tour?'

With that abrupt change of subject came an equally abrupt change of mood. Adam was no longer gazing at her as if he wanted to penetrate her soul. Instead he wore an expression that was pleasant but abstracted, as if he were simply a courteous host, keen to please, but only superficially interested in the discussion. Caroline had the uncomfortable sense that she was really rather a nuisance to him.

'Look, you don't have to show me around,' she insisted. 'I can perfectly well drive myself, if you have other things to do.'

'No, it's all right,' he said blandly. 'I don't mind.'

And, with that, he put one large, firm hand between her shoulderblades and propelled her firmly towards the car park.

'You'll find its quite an attractive city,' he said, as he helped her into the car.

As they drove around the gleaming streets of Canberra, Caroline had to admit that Adam was right. The whole place had a manicured look so that she could almost imagine people coming out at night with nail scissors and little scrubbing brushes to keep all the gardens so neat and tidy. Yet she found it hard to concentrate on the features that Adam was pointing out to her—the gleaming jet of the carillon water spout in the lake, flashing like a river of diamonds in the winter sun, the new Houses of Parliament with their huge metal flagpole, the fascinating diversity of the various foreign embassies built in their own national styles, the angular architecture of the National Gallery. For, to her dismay, she found herself quite incapable of thinking about anything except Adam himself. Was he thawing towards her? Did she even want him to? What did she feel towards him? Dressed in his immaculate Canberra suit and tie, he seemed completely unrelated to the man who had swept her into such an ecstasy of passion only a few days earlier. In fact it was almost impossible to believe that they had done such things together. A wave of embarrassment flooded through Caroline and she wished fervently that she could forget the whole episode. Yet at the same time she felt a perverse annoyance at the ease with which Adam had evidently forgotten it. Or had he? She darted a furtive glance at him, but he was looking through the windscreen at the road ahead.

'Would you like to see the Botanic Gardens?' he asked. 'Normally I'd think it was too cold to take a visitor there in winter, but in view of your occupation you might like to risk it.'

'Yes, I'll risk it,' she agreed with a sigh.

The words 'visitor' and 'occupation' echoed bitterly in her ears. Had Adam chosen them deliberately to remind her that she had no real place in his life? It was true enough, after all. She was nothing but a professional botanist, merely passing through Adam's territory and encountering him in the course of her work. It would be madness to think anything more might come of it.

It was cold in the Botanic Gardens, but the sky was so dazzlingly blue and the sunshine so bright that she scarcely cared. The air was as chill and invigorating as sparkling white wine, and her spirits lifted again.

'I love the smell of Australia,' she said, sniffing joyfully. 'There's something about the scent of eucalypts that's so piercing and aromatic. You must miss it when you leave the country.'

'I do,' Adam agreed. 'I was working in China a few years ago and I drove into a village that had a plantation of gum trees near a field. I stopped the car just so that I could get out and smell them.'

'China?' echoed Caroline. 'What on earth were you doing there?'

'This and that,' he replied vaguely. 'Nothing that really matters to me now.'

She stopped dead and stared at him in exasperation. 'You're infuriating,' she complained. 'You've wormed just about every bit of information imaginable out of me—my childhood, my marriage, my career. And yet you really don't give much in return. Oh, you've told me about your schooldays and your plans for the station, but there seems to be a huge gap in between. It's as if nothing exists for you if it didn't happen at Winnamurra.'

Adam frowned thoughtfully.

'There's a certain amount of truth in that,' he admitted. 'But why does it bother you?'

Caroline shrugged and walked on. By now they were in a fern glade amid the sound of rushing water and the dank smell of primeval vegetation. Down here the sunlight penetrated only in thin shafts and there were patches of ice on the path so that she had to watch her step. This only served to increase her frustration.

'I don't know,' she said irritably. 'But it makes me feel as if you're shutting me out, as if you don't want me to make friends with you or be able to make any kind of claim on you.'

She paused and looked at him expectantly, half hoping that he would deny it. But Adam's blue eyes narrowed as if he were thinking over her words.

'Perhaps you're right,' he admitted at last. 'But I wasn't really thinking of it in those terms. The main reason I don't talk about the past is that I've made a choice about how I want to live. And I'd rather look forward than back. Perhaps you'd be wise to do the same thing.'

She gave him a startled glance.

'Are you talking about Jeremy?' she asked, forgetting to keep her eyes on the glassy path.

Suddenly her feet shot from under her and she gasped. But before she could fall, Adam's powerful arms came around her and steadied her.

'Yes, I'm talking about Jeremy,' he murmured.

And, tilting her chin in his hand, he kissed her very gently on the lips. Her heart thudded wildly and she stared into his eyes, which were as blue as the cold sky behind them. Their breath mingled in the frosty air and Caroline felt a soaring sense of exhilaration inside her. Only one interpretation of Adam's words seemed possible to her—that he wanted her to forget the past so that she could share a future with him. Swallowing hard, she smiled hesitantly at him.

'Do you really think it's important for me to put the past behind me?' she asked earnestly.

'I think it's the most important thing you can possibly do,' replied Adam.

CHAPTER SIX

IT WAS bitterly cold when Alf came to pick them up that evening. Overhead the stars blazed out, white and frosty, against a navy blue sky. Haloes of light clung around the street lamps and their footsteps rang on the cobble-stoned driveway. Caroline was waiting with barely concealed impatience for the dinner to begin. All day she had been consumed by excitement and curiosity as she tried to work out what sort of game Adam was playing with her. After their brief, heady embrace in the deserted Botanic Gardens, he had returned with maddening swiftness to his usual inscrutable manner. Although he had agreed that they should get to know each other better, he had taken obvious delight in tantalising her. Telling her that he wanted to remain a man of mystery a little longer, he had refused to give anything away. To all her questions about his past life he had simply replied, 'My friends will enlighten you soon enough,' and refused to offer any further clues. As the car sped towards the shores of Lake Burley Griffin, Caroline made one final effort to crack his obstinate silence on the matter.

'Will there be many people at this dinner?' she asked lightly.

There was a moment's pause before he answered.

'No. Five couples including us.'

She fumed silently at the amusement in his tone. 'But who are they?' she persisted.

'Just some old friends of mine. You'll meet them soon enough.'

She could get no more out of him, but soon the limousine turned into the road leading along the shores

112

of Lake Burley Griffin and drew up next to a brilliantly lit building.

'Here we are, sir,' said Alf, reverting to his formal manner. 'The Lakeside Hotel.'

Jumping nimbly out of the car, the chauffeur came around to their side and helped Caroline out of the vehicle. Then he stood respectfully at attention while Adam followed her on to the pavement.

'I hope you have a very pleasant evening, sir,' he said. 'Will you want me to wait for you?'

'No, don't bother, Alf,' replied Adam. 'Mr Sloane will be at the dinner and he can give us a ride home. No point keeping two drivers hanging about, is there?'

As the car pulled away, a uniformed hotel employee came forward to usher them into the building.

'Good evening, Mr Fletcher; good evening, Dr Faircroft,' he said. 'Your private dining-room overlooking the lake is ready for you, but perhaps you'd like to come into the Lawson Room for drinks first. May I take your coats for you?'

Caroline's lambswool jacket and Adam's black overcoat were whisked away and they found themselves following the young man down a thickly carpeted corridor. Knocking at a door, he stepped inside.

'Dr Caroline Faircroft and Mr Fletcher are here, Minister.'

Minister? thought Caroline in bewilderment as she stepped forward into the room. Whatever does he mean? She had a jumbled impression of soft lighting, potted palms and subdued background music, then a man of about Adam's age with auburn hair rose from the depths of a leather armchair and came to meet them.

'G'day, Adam,' he said. 'How's it going, mate?'

Then he turned to Caroline and shook her hand warmly.

'Hello, Caroline,' he continued. 'I'm an old friend of Adam's, so I hope you won't want to stand on ceremony with me. My name's Mark Sloane, I'm the Minister for

Trade. And this is Priscilla Townsend, my research assistant.'

A tall, curvaceous brunette in a figure-hugging red dress set down her glass on the bar and lounged towards them with tigerish grace.

'How do you do, Caroline?' she purred, extending two fingers in a token handshake.

Yet although she addressed Caroline, she did not bother listening to her reply. Indeed, her eyes never left Adam's face. Caroline was conscious immediately of a powerful undercurrent of tension between the two. She saw Adam's mouth tighten and a muscle twitched sharply at his temple. Standing on tiptoe, Priscilla kissed him fleetingly on the cheek.

'Hello, darling,' she trilled. 'How lovely to see you again so soon. I wasn't expecting you for at least another two weeks. Did it get boring up there in the outback?'

'No,' replied Adam shortly. 'I'm surprised to see you here, Priscilla. I thought you were in Indonesia.'

'Was, darling, was,' corrected Priscilla. 'I've been back for the last ten days.'

'Caroline, can I get you a drink from the bar?' asked Adam abruptly.

'Gin and tonic, please,' muttered Caroline.

She felt horribly out of her depth, as if she had just walked into the middle of a family row without having a clue as to what was going on. Glancing up, she surprised a look of wry sympathy on Mark Sloane's face.

'Have you known Adam long, Mark?' she asked.

'More than twenty years. We started boarding-school together when we were twelve years old.'

'Oh, boarding-school!' pouted Priscilla. 'Don't talk to me about boarding school. I went to a perfectly foul one in Surrey—Glanville Towers. I expect you've heard of it, Caroline? It was supposed to be one of the best girls' schools in England, but I don't think I had a decent meal the entire time I was there.'

'Are you English?' asked Caroline in surprise.

Priscilla laughed.

'Goodness, no!' she replied. 'People always think that because of my accent. After all, I spent eight years there at the most formative stage of my life. No, no, I'm Australian, but Daddy was a diplomat, you see. And one can hardly drag one's children from country to country every three years, can one?'

'No, one can't,' agreed Adam grimly, appearing at Caroline's side with her drink.

'Yes, well, that was one of the reasons Adam gave up his career as a diplomat, wasn't it, mate? Too much travelling?' commented Mark.

Caroline almost reeled with shock as she took the frosty glass from Adam's fingers.

'You were a diplomat?' she breathed, looking into his glittering, blue eyes.

'Yes,' he replied curtly. 'I spent eleven years in the service.'

Caroline would have liked to question him about his experiences, but it was painfully obvious that Adam was no longer paying attention to her. His gaze was fixed on Priscilla and there was a stormy expression on his face. At that moment there was a flurry of activity at the door. The young hotel employee stepped inside and cleared his throat.

'The Minister for Primary Industry and Mrs Brophy. Mr Kasihiro Toyama and Dr Judith Wallace. Mr and Mrs Robert Pritchard.'

Caroline stared in bewilderment as a group of people led by a genial-looking silver-haired man surged into the room. Within moments she was shaking hands with all of them in swift succession and her head was whirling with details about the Board of Trade and the price of meat in Tokyo. Caroline didn't know much about Australia, but even in London she had seen photos of the Australian newspaper magnate Rob Pritchard splashed across the Sunday newspapers. It shocked her to realise that Adam moved in such exalted circles and

seemed perfectly at home there. His brief flash of temper
on meeting Priscilla had vanished totally and he was now
mingling with the new arrivals, chatting and smiling. Yet
Caroline had the uneasy feeling that some powerful
emotion was seething just below the surface, and she
wondered what was brewing. But, before she had time
to collect her startled thoughts, she found herself deep
in a leather sofa chatting to Mrs Pritchard about her
holiday home in Majorca. Out of the corner of her eye
she saw Adam nursing a glass of Scotch on the rocks
and conversing animatedly with Mr Toyama. To her disbelief she realised that the entire conversation was being
conducted in Japanese.

'Well, I'd better get up and mingle, my dear,' said
Mrs Pritchard, rising lightly to her feet. 'It's been a
pleasure talking to you. You and Adam must come to
dinner with us next time you're in Canberra. Rob thinks
very highly of Adam, you know. He's such a charming
man, and his grasp of international affairs is utterly
brilliant.'

Caroline was left gaping, but fortunately at that
moment dinner was announced and they all filed into
an adjoining dining-room. The Minister for Primary
Industry was seated at one end of the table with Mr
Toyama on his right, the interpreter Judith Wallace on
his left and the only other Japanese speaker, Adam, next
to Judith. Priscilla was sitting opposite Adam, and
Caroline found herself sandwiched between Adam and
Mark. The Pritchards were at the other end of the table
near the Minister's wife. This arrangement was convenient for language reasons, but it also gave Caroline
a very clear view of the byplay among the guests.

· The menu had obviously been chosen to display the
finest Australian produce to best advantage. Tasmanian
smoked salmon was followed by a choice of seafood and
fresh vegetable soups, a main course of grilled lobster
or tender pink fillet steak accompanied by a julienne of
vegetables. And the meal was concluded with an array

of luscious tropical fruits, a platter of assorted cheeses, homemade chocolates and fresh coffee. Along with each course there was a lavish selection of fine Australian wines. Caroline thoroughly enjoyed the excellent food and sparkling conversation. Yet she also found that she was intensely conscious of all the undercurrents that were rippling beneath the surface. Priscilla was flirting subtly with Adam and working her way through a surprising amount of wine. Adam seemed to be exerting his utmost efforts to charm Mr Toyama and Mr Brophy was watching with a shrewd, thoughtful smile as the atmosphere became more and more relaxed and the jokes flew back and forth. When the party finally broke up and the women rose to leave the dining-room, Caroline saw the Minister and Judith Wallace exchange a swift, meaningful glance.

Later, as they were milling around in the foyer of the hotel, Judith looked around the circle of people and smiled.

'It seems a shame to break up the party now,' she said. 'Unfortunately the Minister for Primary Industry and his wife have another engagement tonight, but I'd be delighted if the rest of you could come back to my place for more coffee.'

Back at Judith's house the mood of the gathering became even more relaxed. They drank coffee and liqueurs, listened to some favourite CDs, and Mr Toyama, who was a gifted amateur pianist, played several Haydn piano sonatas followed by some lively jazz. Before long they were all letting their hair down and dancing exuberantly to the music. Even the shrill tone of Judith's whistling kettle didn't disrupt the party. Adam volunteered to go and make Japanese tea, Priscilla disappeared to the bathroom and the others kept dancing. Until a particularly lively sweep of Mark's arm knocked a glass off a bookshelf, spattering Caroline's dress with port.

'Squirt it with some soda water,' urged Judith. 'There are half a dozen bottles in the kitchen fridge. Shall I come and show you?'

'No, don't bother. I'll find it,' said Caroline.

The uproar from the living-room was so loud that nobody heard her enter the kitchen. She pushed open the door—and stopped dead in surprise. Adam was backed against a cupboard with Priscilla twined all over him kissing him passionately. For an instant Caroline was riveted to the spot with shock, then a flaming torrent of emotions surged through her—anger, disbelief, pure molten jealousy. For the first time she realised clearly that she had begun to think of Adam as hers. She made a low, choking sound deep in her throat. Adam drew up his head in shock and his blue eyes met hers. For a long moment they stared at each other in mute accusation and challenge, then Caroline smiled contemptuously.

'Don't let me interrupt anything,' she said through gritted teeth. 'I'll just get some soda water for these stains, then I'll leave you two lovebirds in peace.'

Priscilla raised her head. Her eyes looked smoky and slightly dazed, but they smouldered with unmistakable hostility as they met Caroline's.

'Yes, why don't you?' she demanded. And she nestled dreamily back against Adam's shoulder.

'Come on, Priscilla. I'll take you home now,' he ordered curtly.

'Oh, what a good idea, darling!' she replied with a flirtatious giggle. Caroline gaped. 'But you came with me!' she protested.

'Mark will see you safely home,' Adam assured her. 'I'll speak to him on our way out.'

Before Caroline could say another word, Adam steered Priscilla into the living-room and approached the hostess.

'Sorry to spoil the fun, Judith,' he said with a lazy smile. 'But Priscilla and I will have to be going now.

Duty calls rather early tomorrow morning, I'm afraid. But thanks for a very pleasant time.'

'Yes, thank you, Judith,' echoed Priscilla.

It was the signal for a general move. The Pritchards stopped dancing and began to murmur about getting home, Mark glanced at his watch and Mr Toyama, who was enjoying himself, looked disappointed. In a moment they were all milling around in the hall, exchanging farewells and looking for their coats.

As she reached up to take her jacket, Priscilla tripped on a join in the carpet and lurched rather violently. Adam's hand shot out from nowhere to steady her.

'Oops!' she cried with a shrill giggle. 'Lucky you were there, Tarzan!'

'Yes, it's hard to see where you're walking, isn't it?' agreed Adam. 'Well, goodnight, everyone. Mark, you'll take Caroline home, won't you?'

'Yes, of course,' said Mark with a thoughtful frown.

Caroline was seething with resentment as they walked out to the waiting car, but Mark bent his head and murmured in her ear,

'Just keep your cool. We'll talk about this at home.'

Somehow Caroline managed to control herself until the chauffeur pulled up the government car in the driveway of Adam's house. But the moment the red taillights vanished down the street, all her annoyance boiled over.

'Honestly, how rude!' she exclaimed as Mark opened the front door and waved her into the hall. 'I didn't think even Adam Fletcher would be gross enough to arrive at a party with one woman and take a different one home.'

Mark winced.

'I know you must be annoyed about this,' he admitted. 'But I'm sure Adam had a good reason for it.'

'You're taking it very calmly!' retorted Caroline. 'Does he often snatch your girlfriends from under your nose?'

'Priscilla isn't my girlfriend!' he protested. 'I'm a happily married man with a wife and three kids back in my electorate in North Queensland. Priscilla's only my research assistant. She was on the staff of the previous Minister and she's perfectly competent at her job, so I saw no reason to fire her. But I never really liked her even when she was engaged to Adam.'

'When she was what?' echoed Caroline in a horrified voice.

They stared at each other warily.

'Engaged,' repeated Mark. 'Didn't Adam tell you?'

'No,' admitted Caroline at last. 'But I wish you would. I don't have the faintest idea what's going on here.'

He sighed.

'It's a bit complicated,' he said. 'Come and I'll explain.'

When they were sitting in the living-room, he gave her a shrewd, measuring glance.

'So what do you want to know?' he asked.

Caroline bit her lip.

'As much as you can tell me,' she said frankly. 'Who Priscilla Townsend is, for a start, and what she means to Adam.'

Mark shrugged.

'Well, they met in Japan about four years ago,' he told her. 'Priscilla's father was the Australian Ambassador there and Adam was First Secretary at the Embassy.'

'First Secretary?' echoed Caroline in disbelief.

'Yes, he was a very successful career diplomat until he decided to give it all up and return to the outback. By then he was engaged to Priscilla, but she took one look at Winnamurra Station and broke off the engagement. I don't think it was ever really Adam that she wanted. It was just the glitter of the diplomatic life—foreign postings, cocktail parties, important people coming and going, that sort of thing. It's about two years now since they split up.'

'They didn't look as if they were split up tonight,' pointed out Caroline moodily. 'Adam took her home, didn't he?'

Mark gave a wry smile.

'Out of a sense of duty, if you ask me,' he replied. 'I don't know whether you noticed it, but Priscilla was packing away a fair bit of wine tonight. Adam probably felt she was on the verge of making an embarrassing scene and wanted to get her out of there. He couldn't afford to lose face in front of Mr Toyama. He's busy negotiating a very important beef contract with Japan right now.'

Caroline stared at him.

'So Adam still works for the Government?' she asked slowly.

'Yes, although only on a contract basis these days. He's one of our most valuable consultants on foreign trade. If he wanted to make a full-time career of it, he could move back to Canberra tomorrow, but he won't. He's too committed to Winnamurra.'

Caroline cleared her throat.

'You don't think he might make things up with Priscilla and come back to Canberra?' she demanded.

Mark shook his head emphatically.

'Not a hope,' he replied. 'Adam's a very proud man and he can be pretty unforgiving. He felt that Priscilla's leaving humiliated him, and I'm damned sure he won't give her a second chance.'

Caroline was silent, turning over all that she had learnt. Obviously Adam Fletcher was a far more complex man than she had ever dreamt. And far more of a high flier. Only this morning he had held her in his arms at the Botanic Gardens and she had thought he was inviting her to make a fresh start with him. But was that really likely? In view of the sophisticated crowd he mixed with, wasn't it far more probable that he had only been indulging in an idle flirtation? A feeling of despondency swept through her. Biting her lip, she stared miserably down at the Persian carpet.

'Look,' said Mark, 'I know this is none of my business, but I'd have to be blind not to see that there's something going on between you and Adam. Well, all I want to say is this, Caroline. Give him a chance. He's a fine bloke, and I should know. We were at school and university together, he's godfather to my eldest child and we've shared this house for years on and off. And I know this much about him. He's got his faults, he's hot-tempered and doesn't open up easily about his feelings, but he's not the kind of man to have two women on a string at the same time. If he's got some kind of relationship going with you, there's no way he'd be having an affair with Priscilla at the same time. I'm sure of it.'

Caroline thought of that long, sensual kiss she had witnessed in Judith Wallace's kitchen and her mouth tightened sceptically.

'Are you?' she retorted. 'Well, it's loyal of you to defend him, Mark, but you're wasting your breath. It really doesn't matter to me one way or the other whether Adam is sleeping with Priscilla!'

And that's one of the biggest lies I've ever told, she thought an hour later as she lay wide awake and staring into the darkness. It was after three a.m. and, although she had strained her ears whenever a rare car came down the street, none of them had ever turned into the driveway. There could be little doubt that Adam was spending the night at Priscilla's place. And, in spite of her defiant statement, that knowledge unleashed a storm of contradictory emotions in Caroline's heart—jealousy, yearning, anger, regret. She had always been aware of Adam's aura of virile animal magnetism, but until now she had resolutely repressed her feelings. Now they rose to the surface in a surge of primitive pain and desire. She wanted Adam to possess her, body and soul, to slake the urgent, throbbing need that was uncoiling deep within her. And yet she also wanted to slap his face, to shout

and scream and vent her fury at his betrayal. How dared
he make love to Priscilla Townsend when only a few
days ago Caroline had been the one in his arms? Didn't
he have any scruples whatsoever? If only Adam had had
more patience! He should have recognised the hesitant
unfolding of Caroline's response to him and given her
more time. Instead he had immediately sought satisfaction in another woman's bed, which just showed how
shallow his feelings for Caroline were. And why had he
kissed her only this morning if she meant nothing to him
at all? Burrowing deep into the blankets, she pounded
the pillow angrily with her fists and let out a low groan.

'I hate you, Adam Fletcher!' she breathed. 'I'll never
forgive you for this as long as I live!'

It was nearly noon the following day when he came
home. Caroline was sitting in the living-room, pretending to read a magazine, but actually staring out of
the window. Mark had left a couple of hours earlier for
Parliament and the house was silent—so silent that she
heard the scrape of Adam's key in the front door with
perfect clarity. His footsteps approached the living-room
and Caroline felt her heart thudding violently. Then the
door opened.

'Good morning,' drawled Adam.

Her gaze rose slowly. He was no longer wearing the
dinner suit of the previous evening, but was dressed in
a dark blue business suit, white shirt and grey and navy
tie. A slow surge of anger swept through her. So he even
keeps a change of clothes at Priscilla's place! she thought
fiercely. How convenient! Yet there was no sign of annoyance in her voice when she spoke.

'Good morning,' she retorted coolly. 'I hope you slept
well.'

A glint of amusement flashed in his eyes at her faint
emphasis on the word 'slept'.

'Actually I didn't sleep at all,' he remarked.

Caroline's fragile self-control shattered.

'So what did you do?' she flared. 'Or shouldn't I ask?'

'I took Priscilla Townsend home to bed,' replied Adam deliberately, watching her through narrowed eyes.

'I see,' she sneered.

'Do you?' he drawled. 'I wonder. All I've said so far is that I took her home to bed. I didn't say whether I joined her there or not.'

'Did you?' demanded Caroline. To her annoyance there was a catch in her voice.

'Would it matter to you if I did?' asked Adam, still watching her closely.

'No!' she stormed, leaping to her feet and rushing blindly across to the window.

'You're a hopeless liar!' he growled, following her across the room. She felt his warm grip on her shoulders as he swung her round to face him.

'Take your hands off me!' she hissed.

With exaggerated deliberation he released her.

'Why are you so angry?' he asked. 'Could it be that you're jealous?'

'Don't be absurd!' she exclaimed. 'I just think it's jolly rude for you to invite me out to dinner and then go home with somebody else.'

Adam ran his fingers through his thick blond hair with a harassed gesture.

'Yes, you're right,' he agreed. 'I'm sorry. I wasn't expecting Priscilla to be there, and it was rather awkward the way things turned out.'

'Awkward? You didn't seem to find it in the least bit awkward! And if you think it makes it better that you spent the night with her on impulse, then obviously our values are poles apart and there's no point talking any further!'

'Don't you want to hear my explanation?' snapped Adam.

For a moment Caroline wavered. Then she remembered the scores of threadbare explanations she had heard from Jeremy before he finally came into the open and admitted that he was seeing other women.

'No,' she said, tossing her head. 'What does it matter to me why you're sleeping with your ex-fiancée?'

A bleak smile played around the corners of Adam's mouth as he stared at her.

'Interesting how you're so ready to believe the worst of me,' he murmured. 'So I'm still sleeping with Priscilla, am I?'

'Well, aren't you?' parried Caroline. 'Why else would you stay with her for the entire night?'

He gritted his teeth.

'I stayed at Priscilla's because she had something rather important she wanted to discuss with me,' he replied evenly.

'Oh, yes?' said Caroline. 'What, exactly? Or is it a private matter?'

His blue eyes held hers and his voice was deep and very serious when he replied. 'Yes, it is rather,' he agreed. 'But perhaps you ought to know it anyway. She wants to renew our engagement.'

'What?' Caroline felt as shocked as if the ground had suddenly opened beneath her feet. 'W-what did you say to her?' she stuttered.

Adam gave her a long, searching look.

'Anyone would think you really cared,' he remarked scornfully. 'But you don't, do you?'

She felt an agonising urge to burst into tears, but she held on grimly to the only thing left to her—her pride.

'Not particularly,' she said with a shrug. 'We've had a rather pleasant flirtation, Adam, but your marriage plans are nothing to do with me. I'm just not interested in that sort of thing. As I told you before, I'm a career woman. And the only thing I want to do now is collect my fire lilies and get back to London.'

Three days later Danny Japulula phoned to say that the tribal elders had returned from their walkabout. Not long after, Caroline and Adam flew back to the cattle station. On the surface they were polite enough, but deep down their mutual suspicion and resentment was fiercer than ever. Caroline had come to an aching realisation while she was in Canberra. She knew now that she was more than half in love with Adam, and the knowledge infuriated her. The last thing she wanted was to be in love with some complete swine who wouldn't even tell her whether he was now engaged to another woman or not. As for Adam, he treated her with a distant courtesy that was even more wounding than their previous quarrels.

On the evening of their return, Adam led her down the dirt road that led from the homestead towards the cluster of bungalows opposite the stockyards. But before they reached the houses, he veered off on to a path that led them through the darkness to a large, blazing fire under some huge gum trees. As they stepped into the red glow of the firelight, Caroline saw that eight or nine elderly men were sitting cross-legged in a circle around the fire. They were dressed only in shorts and most of them had grizzled hair and beards that showed startlingly white against their dark skin. With one accord they all turned grave dark eyes to examine her as she stepped hesitantly into the light.

Disconcerted by this frank appraisal, she stared helplessly up at Adam.

'What do I do?' she whispered.

'Most of them don't speak English very well,' he told her. 'So you'd better let me do the talking. I've already told them basically what you want, but they may want to ask you some questions, and I'll interpret for you.'

Looking completely at home, he squatted down in the dust and gave the men a wide, friendly smile. Then he began to talk in a strange, guttural language. There were nods and questions and a good deal of animated discussion. Once again the old men turned to examine Caroline critically, and one of them rose to his feet and padded softly across to stare into her eyes, before returning to his place in the dust. After several minutes of this, silence descended on the group.

'Well?' prompted Caroline eagerly.

'You're in luck,' Adam told her. 'Charlie Yunupingu says you have a kind face and he thinks you can be trusted. He doesn't believe you had anything to do with the theft of the painting. And they're all very keen to help the sick children in any way they can. They say that provided you have an escort to the sacred site, you can collect as much material as you like, consistent with leaving reasonable breeding stocks of the plant in place.'

'That's wonderful!' she exclaimed. Her face lit up and her eyes shone with excitement like those of a child on Christmas Eve.

'There's only one snag,' warned Adam.

'What?' she demanded urgently. 'What is it?'

'The tribesmen say that you've no chance of transplanting mature fire lilies successfully. They'll simply die. If you want to propagate the plants successfully, you'll have to wait another two months until they set seed.'

Her disappointment was so acute that she let out a low gasp of dismay. Two more months! She would have to go back to Darwin and spend two months kicking her heels doing nothing, waiting until the seeds were ready. And then she would have to persuade Adam to allow her to come back and collect them. She pressed her lips together, trying to stop them from quivering.

'I see,' she said with dignity. 'Well, it's a disappointment, of course, but I shan't give up. Please thank the tribal elders very, very much for me, Adam. I'm really honoured that they trusted me. And thank you too, for... everything.'

Her throat tightened and she had to take a deep, slow breath to steady her. After a moment she gave a small, tense smile and continued.

'Naturally I won't trespass on your hospitality any longer, Adam. I'll get a lift to Darwin as soon as I can, but if you'd let me come back and collect the seeds in October——'

She got no further. Adam seized her by the shoulders and stared down into her miserable face.

'Don't be ridiculous!' he exclaimed. 'If you need to stay on for another two months, then you'll just have to stay here.'

Caroline drew in a long, unsteady breath.

'Thank you,' she said. 'When can we go and visit the site?'

'I'll take you tomorrow,' he said.

The early morning sunlight was striking clear and pale gold across the barren landscape as they drove away the following morning. This time they did not take the track that they had used on their first trip into the bush, but took a different direction instead, a well marked dirt road heading north towards Arnhem Land. Somehow Caroline had been expecting to travel for at least fifty miles, so it came as a complete shock to her when Adam slowed the jeep after half an hour and pointed to some craggy golden rocks barely a hundred yards away.

'That's the site just up there,' he said. 'But I don't want to take the jeep any further in case I wreck the plants, so we'll have to get out and walk now.'

'All right,' she agreed.

Shutting the door, she stood adjusting her camera strap for a moment—luckily she had thought to stock up on film in Canberra—then picked her way across the rocks in Adam's wake. Although the place seemed totally deserted, it was soon apparent that it was teeming with life. Cicadas shrilled in the sun-bleached undergrowth, lizards lay sunning themselves on flat-topped rocks, and a flock of colourful galahs rose shrieking from the canopy of a tall eucalyptus tree at their approach. Adam led her through a wide passage in the rocks and they emerged into a natural amphitheatre, which was knee-deep in flame-coloured wildflowers. A wonderful scent of warm caramel came wafting out to meet them, and Caroline stopped dead, sniffing the air delightedly.

'Fire lilies!' she breathed exultantly. 'Oh, how wonderful, after all this time! And there are simply thousands of them!'

With a whoop of joy, she raced across the red dusty entranceway and flung herself on her knees at the edge of that shimmering orange tapestry of flowers. She was too much of a botanist to crush any of them, but she knelt and buried her face in their nodding petals so that she could inhale their warm, sweet perfume.

'Oh, thank you, Adam!' she cried. 'They're absolutely splendid! I can't tell you how grateful I am.'

In a moment, she was happily taking photographs from every possible angle. Then, unwinding the strap of her shoulder-bag and feverishly scrabbling out the contents, she began to lay out plastic bags for soil samples, along with rulers and a trowel and a notebook. Adam watched her with a thoughtful frown on his face.

'I'm not keeping you away from your work too long, am I?' she asked hesitantly. 'I mean, you could go back to the station and pick me up later if you like.'

'No, I'll stay,' he told her. 'You just do whatever you need to and give me a shout when you're ready to go.'

It was half an hour before Caroline gave a tentative call and waved to him. He came scrambling down from a rocky crag, from which he had been surveying the landscape, and strode across to join her. She came to meet him with a glowing face, a bag bulging with samples and two large fire lilies clutched in a plastic sack against her chest.

'They'll die,' warned Adam. 'They won't transplant successfully, you know.'

'I know,' she admitted with a quirky smile. 'But I can't resist trying, all the same. Besides, I can always dry one and cut up the other for tissue samples to study under the microscope. And I want to write up a description of the whole plant for *The Australian Journal of Botany*. Oh, Adam, I've got heaps of things to do!'

But Adam showed no response to this fervent enthusiasm. Instead he reached out his hands for her samples.

'I'll put this stuff in the jeep for you,' he said in clipped tones.

Caroline's face fell. She was suddenly miserably conscious of how much she had wanted him to share her excitement, to rejoice with her at this extraordinary milestone that she had just reached. Instead there was nothing but blank indifference in his eyes. Biting her lip, she thrust the samples into his hands and turned away. Adam took a step after her, then paused. Tightening his hold on the bags, he hurried down to the jeep and stowed them in the back.

When he returned, he saw that Caroline was sitting in the dust with her knees hunched up and her arms wrapped protectively around them. She did not look up at his approach, but went on staring pensively at the sea of undulating fire lilies. A dreadful feeling of listlessness had overtaken her. For so long she had dreamed and planned and striven for the moment when she would hold the fire lilies in her hands—and, with them, the chance to save thousands of lives. Yet now her triumph was completely spoiled by Adam's surly lack of interest. She felt as if somebody had punched her in the stomach.

'What's the matter?' he demanded.

'Nothing,' she replied bleakly.

'Have you finished what you wanted to do here?'

'Yes.'

But she did not rise to her feet. Adam looked at her with a touch of alarm.

'You're not ill, are you?' he demanded abruptly.

'No, I'm not ill,' sighed Caroline.

He stared at her with a perplexed expression.

'Do you want to have look at the rock paintings before we leave?' he asked.

For the first time a hint of animation showed in her face. Her lips twisted into a wry grin.

'The paintings?' she echoed. 'How extraordinary! I'd forgotten all about them. But yes, I suppose I'd like to see them. Am I allowed, though? I thought women weren't allowed to see sacred objects.'

He shrugged.

'That's true of some things,' he agreed. 'But not these. And anyway, you ought to see the devastation that your precious friend Michael Barclay caused to them.'

'He's not my friend!' she protested. 'I only met the man once.'

'And found him a charming fellow!' sneered Adam.

'Yes, I did!' she retorted. 'And I dare say you did too, or he wouldn't have managed to worm his way into your confidence enough to steal the wretched painting! Anyway, I should imagine a con-man would have to have charm as part of his stock in trade, wouldn't you? But what's that got to do with me?'

Adam flushed darkly but did not reply. He seized her arm.

'Come on,' he ordered. 'They're under that rocky overhang to the west.'

With her chin stuck out and an angry glare on her face, Caroline allowed herself to be dragged around the field of fire lilies to a smoothly flowing formation of rock that jutted gracefully forth on the far side.

'Duck your head,' ordered Adam. 'It's higher once you're inside.'

She blinked as she left the bright sunlight, but in a moment her eyes became used to the dimmer light beneath the overhang and she saw that she was inside a natural shelter perhaps twenty feet long by eight feet wide. The sandstone floor was gritty with yellow dust and the long interior wall was covered with a dramatic array of Aboriginal paintings which flowed smoothly from one end to the other, except for one vicious disfiguration right in the centre. Here a rectangle almost two square metres in size had been hacked away, leaving bare, scarred rock to ruin the design. Caroline padded quietly across and examined the paintings. They were vivid depictions of native animals and hunters in red and white ochre and charcoal black, done in the X-ray style that showed the internal organs of the animals and yet still preserved a lively realism. Kangaroos bounded energetically across the rock face, hunters raised their spears, goannas twisted into shapes full of vitality and fish seemed to swim into crevices in the rock.

'They're incredible!' she exclaimed. 'But how on earth could anybody bear to deface them like that?'

Adam shrugged.

'Greed,' he said succinctly. 'Barclay must have made a packet out of that painting when he sold it to your museum.'

She winced.

'I expect you're right,' she admitted. 'But I'm quite sure the museum would never have bought it if they'd known it was stolen. Couldn't you try to get it returned now that you know where it is?'

'I've already opened negotiations on the matter,' Adam told her. 'But it's a fairly complicated business. And of course, even if we succeed, it will never look quite the same once it's glued back in.'

Caroline fingered the cut edges of stone.

'No, I suppose not,' she said. 'But how on earth did he get it out in the first place? It must have been quite an effort cutting out a piece of stone that size. Especially without attracting attention.'

Adam nodded grimly.

'Yes,' he agreed. 'Mind you, the geology of the place was apparently in his favour. According to a geologist that I consulted, the sandstone layers here are deeply dipping sediments. See how they're tilted on their sides so that the beds are nearly vertical? Evidently the divisions between layers are just like pages in a book and can be split off quite easily with the right equipment. And Barclay had the right equipment. What's more, thanks to my own stupidity, he had plenty of opportunity to use it.'

'What do you mean?' asked Caroline curiously.

Adam scowled.

'Well, it was like this,' he explained. 'He came out here with a lot of video gear and sound equipment and spun me some yarn about how he was doing a documentary on Aboriginal lifestyle for British television. I didn't even check him out, I just rolled out the red carpet and encouraged my stockmen to do the same thing. Once he had our confidence, he drove out here one day with his jeep, but on this occasion he didn't have video equipment in the back. He had a petrol-driven generator and a portable diamond saw. Evidently he didn't stop at the end of the track. He simply drove right over the field of fire lilies, set up his saw, cut out the slab and went for his life. He made a total fool of me and, by heaven, I won't forget it in a hurry! And I'll tell you something else. If this story about extracting some wonder drug from the fire lilies is another one of Barclay's inventions, I'll really make you suffer!'

Caroline flinched at the grim expression on his face.

'You're being utterly ridiculous!' she exclaimed. 'I'm here for one thing and one thing only, Adam: to collect the seeds of the fire lily. And once I've done that, I'll be leaving for London so fast it will make your head spin.'

'I'm glad to hear it,' he said harshly. 'Because the sooner you get out of this place, Caroline, the happier I'll be!'

CHAPTER SEVEN

THE weeks that followed were a difficult time for Caroline. In one respect, she had never been so happy in her life. Her work was progressing rapidly, and each day brought new botanical surprises. As Adam had predicted, the mature fire lilies soon died, but the dried plants were still valuable for study. What was even more exciting was the realisation that she was living in the midst of a botanist's paradise. While they were away in Canberra Adam had given orders for the rest of her equipment from the wrecked jeep to be brought back to the homestead. To her delight, several of the plants she had collected on her expedition into the wilderness proved to be new species previously unknown to science. As a result, she often stayed up until after midnight, drawing diagrams and puzzling over classifications. And when the Aboriginal people on the station realised how keen she was, they did all they could to help. Time after time, Caroline was summoned by a tentative knock at the door to find a shy, dark-eyed child or a smiling, inarticulate woman with a sack full of plants for her inspection. Yet her pleasure in all this was overshadowed by the constant, lurking tension in her dealings with Adam.

There was no longer any physical contact between them, but the old magic was as potent as ever. Caroline found it pure torture to share the house with Adam and was often conscious of his gaze resting silently on her as she moved about the house. Yet there could be no recapturing their earlier intimacy. The thought of Priscilla came between them, and she was not the only barrier. Adam still seemed to harbour a lingering suspicion that Caroline was interested in the rock paintings, and he never questioned her fierce assertion that marriage did not interest her. But in spite of their antagonism a wary companionship grew up between them. Bit by bit Caroline found herself drawn into the daily activities of station life. Adam spent several hilarious mornings teaching her to ride a camel, and then there were boundary riding sessions to practise her new-found skill. She learnt to muster cattle by helicopter and watched with interest as Adam roped and branded the newly yarded beasts. And, although the homestead was so isolated, there were occasional social contacts—the weekly 'galah session'—so-called after the raucous native parrots—when all the women of the far-flung region tuned into their radios for a neighbourly chat. Other cattle station owners sometimes dropped in by helicopter for afternoon tea and, as a matter of courtesy, anyone bound for Darwin on a shopping spree always called in to take orders. On one of these occasions Caroline asked her neighbour Jackie Webb to look out for some pot plants and curtain fabric for her. Jackie returned triumphantly with a collection of fabric ends and house plants, and Caroline set to work to decorate the rather impersonal interior of the homestead. When Adam arrived back from a three-day boundary riding trip, he stared in disbelief.

'I can't believe it!' he exclaimed, gazing around at the colourful curtains, appliquéd cushions and lush green plants. 'You've transformed the place! I always meant to get it decorated eventually, but I've always been too busy with the station work.'

That night over dinner, he asked Caroline's opinion of some wallpaper he had thought of buying, and they soon had their heads together over a collection of home decorating catalogues. It was fun, but warning bells sounded in Caroline's head. There was no point getting too involved in making improvements to the house as if she were a starry-eyed bride, when she knew perfectly well that she would have to leave in a few weeks. As if

to underline her misgivings, Priscilla Townsend chose
that very evening to telephone Adam and have a long
conversation with him. Adam took the call in his office,
and although Caroline's innate sense of decency would
not allow her to listen in on the extension she tormented
herself by wondering what they were saying. The sooner
I leave here, the better, she thought bitterly. And when
Adam finally returned with a look of smug satisfaction
on his face, she took her revenge by babbling about how
much she missed London and longed to be home.

Yet it was completely untrue, and she knew it. The
Northern Territory had cast its strange, primeval spell
over her, and she knew that as long as she lived she would
be haunted by its harsh beauty. Each day, with the greed
of a miser hoarding treasure, she stored up memories
for the future. Memories of golden days spent in the
saddle with the heat scorching from the rocky ridges and
the red plains. Memories of cobalt blue skies and flocks
of shrieking yellow and white cockatoos wheeling
overhead. Memories of rock pools where the cool green
water caressed her skin like silk and ripples of sunlight
danced gaily on the sandstone crags. And, above all,
memories of a tall, blond man with a determined mouth
and the most piercing blue eyes she had ever seen. It
made her sick at heart to think of leaving all this forever,
and yet time was slipping relentlessly away.

August had been hot, and September was hotter still.
Often when they were flying over the herds of Brahmin
cattle in the helicopter, they would see the plumes of
smoke that announced fires lit by natural lightning
strikes. And yet, oddly, the field of fire lilies always
seemed to be miraculously spared. Adam had offered to
set a torch to it, but Caroline always refused. She told
him she was afraid that artificial intervention might ruin
everything, but deep down she knew that her real reason
was quite different. Once the fire lilies dropped their seed,
there would be no further reason for her to stay.

There were times when she longed to blurt out all her feelings to Adam, but one look at that sardonic face was always enough to stop her. Some kind of truce had grown up between them, but it wasn't enough to make Caroline risk the humiliation of laying her pride on the line. She had suffered enough rejection and pain when her marriage ended. There was certainly no point inviting another rebuff. So she continued doggedly on, working hard and chattering pertly about her plans for her future in England. And if an aching sense of emptiness crept through her whenever she thought of a future without Adam Fletcher, she was careful not to let him see it. Yet at last the long-awaited bushfire swept through the field of fire lilies, and she realised that there was no further reason for her to stay.

It was late October, two weeks after the fire, when Adam announced that it was time to collect the fire lily seeds. Ever since the beginning of the month, the weather had been growing steadily more humid and oppressive, and Caroline blamed her low spirits on the sweltering conditions. Yet Adam, who should have been more acclimatised, seemed equally gloomy. On the day they drove out to the plant site, he did his best to help her collect the glossy brown seeds, but his face was set and unsmiling as he worked. And Caroline was acutely conscious of his piercing gaze as she moved among the clumps of blackened plants.

After ten minutes or so, her hair was plastered to her scalp with sweat. But she went on doggedly crawling about, although her back ached, her knees were scratched and her hands were filthy. At last, when she had more than a dozen bags sitting neatly labelled and stapled in a shoebox, Adam rose to his feet and looked down at her with narrowed blue eyes.

'Haven't you got enough?' he asked.

'No. I want to be sure that there are plenty to supply any researchers who may be interested in the project. So

you'll just have to be patient, however hard you may
find that!'

Adam snorted and walked away. Reaching the low-
hanging rock formation that sheltered the paintings, he
stopped dead and swung an exasperated punch at the
rock.

'Don't you ever give up on anything?' he demanded,
swinging around to confront her.

'No,' she retorted, still scrabbling in the dirt. 'I'd crawl
on my hands and knees over broken glass to get these
seeds home safely!'

'You look as if you already did,' said Adam drily.
'Look, Caroline, we can always make another trip
tomor——'

He began walking towards her, but as he did so, something drew his gaze towards the sky and he stopped dead
with a horrified expression on his face. And when he
spoke, it was not about making another trip.

'You're going to have to stop now, whether you like
it or not,' he warned.

'Why?' asked Caroline.

'Because it's going to rain!' he retorted, looking back
at the blue vault overhead.

Her gaze followed his, then she sat back on her heels,
looking puzzled.

'But the sky is absolutely cloudless!' she protested.
'Are you sure?'

'Yes,' insisted Adam. 'I can feel it.'

She was suddenly conscious of a tense feeling of foreboding that settled on her like a shroud. The air felt
warm and heavy and somehow charged with danger. Yet
there was nothing to mar the dazzling blue perfection
of the heavens, except for a distant smudge like a careless
fingermark on a photo. But Adam was staring at this
apprehensively, and his voice was suddenly sharp with
urgency.

'Come on!' he ordered, snatching her hand and
dragging her upright. 'We've got to get out of here fast!'

The movement took her by surprise and her paper bag tore, spilling a fine stream of seeds on the ground.

'Damn!' she exclaimed, bending to pick them up.

'You don't have time for that!' roared Adam. 'Drop them!'

With a ruthless sweep of the arm, he struck the torn bag out of her hand, snatched up the laden shoebox from the ground and began to sprint across the fire-blackened ground.

'Come on!' he yelled over his shoulder. 'Run for your life!'

By the time they reached the jeep, Caroline's breath was coming in long, burning gasps and her hair was flying. Adam already had her door open, and as she flung herself into her seat, he immediately began reversing hastily back on to the track.

'What's the hurry?' she panted.

'This track floods in the Wet,' he replied curtly. 'If we don't get home now, the jeep could be stuck out here for months. Not only that. There's a dry creek bed between us and the homestead. If that floods before we get to it, we've had it. It'll be too dangerous to cross, and it's a two-hundred-mile walk to get around it. So hold on to your seat, because I'm about to break the land-speed record!'

Branches of lightning soon began to split the sky, and they were barely a mile down the track, hurtling along at a terrifying pace, when Caroline heard the first thunder. Like some gigantic bowling ball rumbling down an alley, it rolled towards them and crashed around them with a huge reverberation of sound.

'Oh, hell,' groaned Adam, stepping on the accelerator.

It was frightening and yet wildly exhilarating to try to outrun the storm. By now the sky was growing ominously dark and huge armies of black clouds were massing overhead. Lightning ripped across the sky in brilliant traceries and the low ripple and growl of thunder was suddenly joined by the spatter of raindrops across the bonnet of the jeep.

'Come on, come on,' urged Adam, hunching over the wheel and crooning to the vehicle as if it were a restive horse.

Caroline glanced across at him and saw the blaze of excitement in his speedwell-blue eyes, the taut, determined thrust of his chin, the daredevil look of glee that lit his features.

'You're enjoying every moment of this!' she said accusingly.

'Why not?' he countered, swinging the wheel and sending the jeep hurtling wildly round a bend. 'I like the odd bit of danger. It makes me feel alive!'

A strange sensation of breathlessness seized her. Her slender hands clenched into fists and she watched him with her lips parted and her eyes shining. Yes, you are alive, she thought fiercely. More vividly, turbulently alive than anybody I've ever known before. And you make me feel alive too. Oh, Adam, I'm so glad I came here and met you, whatever happens.

'Well, do you think we'll make it across the creek before the storm breaks?' he demanded challengingly.

'Before it breaks?' echoed Caroline in a puzzled voice, looking at the windscreen wipers swishing back the curtain of rain. 'It's already broken, hasn't it?'

'Oh, no, sweetheart,' murmured Adam softly. 'This is just the prelude. And you'd better pray that we get there before it does break.'

Rain swept down on them in a steady stream and the sky was so full of loud, ear-splitting cracks, long, reverberating rumbles and blinding flashes of light that it seemed as if some aerial battle was being fought overhead. And when they finally came lurching through a series of red, soupy puddles to the 'dry' creek bed they had crossed a few hours earlier, they found it was covered in swiftly flowing orange water.

'Oh, no!' wailed Caroline. 'Whatever shall we do?'

Adam's face was screwed into a frown of concentration as he leaned out of the window and examined a white pole with black markings that projected from the waters. Then, with scarcely a pause, he drove straight in. Caroline flinched as she felt the flood waters surging around the wheels of the vehicle and heard the steady roar of the rising torrent, but Adam's judgement was sound. The bottom stayed reassuringly firm beneath them, and after a few heart-stopping moments, they found themselves lurching up the muddy slope of the opposite bank.

'Oh, thank goodness,' breathed Caroline.

'We'll be all right now,' Adam assured her. 'It's easy going from here on.'

Yet the drama was not quite over. Already the track to the homestead was covered in huge, spreading puddles that sent up showers of dirty water as the jeep sped through them. And as they reached the final section which led from the stockyards to the house, the storm broke in its full fury. To Caroline the rain had already seemed heavy, but now it came hurtling against the windshield with all the force of a fire hose spraying in violent gusts. Squalls of wind made the jeep plunge wildly, veering towards the roadside verge, so that Adam had to fight to keep it on course. It was impossible to see more than a few feet ahead in the driving rain, except when a flash of lightning blazed across the sky, briefly illuminating the tossing foliage of the peppercorn trees. The windshield wipers could make no headway in the steady torrent that poured over them and Adam had to lean out the window and peer into the darkness that loomed ahead of them. Within a couple of minutes he was completely soaked and rain was buffeting into every corner of the jeep's interior.

'There's the shed!' he shouted above the uproar of the storm, and swung the wheel.

The sudden silence was deafening. Climbing out of the jeep, Caroline found herself in the dark, cavernous interior of the metal building amid the smells of diesel oil and cattle dip. But as she recovered her breath, she realised that the place was not so silent as she thought. Overhead the rain was hurtling on to the tin roof with the monotonous fury of machine-gun fire. Adam came round the front of the vehicle to meet her.

'Well, are you ready to make a break for the house?' he asked casually, as if this sort of uproar were normal.

She looked startled.

'Shouldn't we wait until the rain stops?' she asked.

He grinned suddenly, his teeth showing white and even in the gloom.

'Not unless you're planning on camping out here for a couple of days,' he said. 'Once it starts to come down, the rain can go on for a very long time.'

Caroline stared apprehensively out at the waterfall that was pouring down outside the double doors of the shed.

'What about the fire lily seeds?' she asked.

'Leave them here. They'll have more chance of staying dry in the jeep. Now, when I say "Go!", make a run for the stairs. OK?'

'OK,' she replied breathlessly.

He led her to the open doors and his hand rested briefly on her shoulder.

'Go!' he shouted.

She launched herself into that terrifying world of violence. A thousand missiles of rain hurtled down on her and the sheer force of the wind sent her reeling on her feet. Lightning flashed against the darkness of the sky, lighting up the silhouette of the house, and she ducked her head and set off in a stumbling run towards the stairs. Long before she reached them, she was soaked to the skin and blinded by rain. But as she set her foot on the bottom step, a strong arm came round her and she found herself half carried, half dragged up to the front door.

A moment later they were inside, both completely drenched. Caroline stared about her in a dazed fashion and realised that water was streaming off her into a puddle on the floor.

'Oh, no!' she exclaimed. 'I'll ruin the polished floor. I must get a cloth for it.'

'Leave it!' ordered Adam impatiently. 'Just go into your room and strip your clothes off.'

She blinked, still too overwhelmed by the buffeting of the storm to make any sense of his instructions.

'Well, don't just stand there,' he growled. 'Get yourself dried and dressed, you silly girl. Never mind about the floor.'

Caroline took a hesitant step towards the hall and saw that she was leaving a trail of water on the polished boards. She stopped doubtfully. With an exclamation of impatience, Adam put a ruthless hand between her shoulder blades and propelled her forcibly through the door and down the hall to her bedroom. Flinging open the door, he thrust her none too gently across the floor and into the bathroom.

'Dry yourself!' he ordered, thrusting a towel into her hands.

Yet somehow the buffeting of the storm seemed to have addled her wits. She simply stood there hopelessly, blinking as the rain streamed down her face and holding the towel as if it were something unfamiliar. With an exclamation of impatience, Adam snatched it from her hands and began briskly drying her wet hair. His movements were so vigorous that he knocked her off balance so that she staggered and almost fell.

'Sorry!' he exclaimed, clutching her arm.

She looked up at him with rain-fringed grey eyes, and for an instant time stood still. The harsh, uneven sound of Adam's breathing filled the room, then the towel slipped from his fingers. Caroline stared at him with her eyes full of yearning and her lips parted. Her breasts rose and fell with her sudden, sharp intake of breath. Seizing her face between his hands, he bent his head and kissed her so violently that her ears rang and the room seemed to spin beneath her feet. She caught at his arms to steady herself and found she could not let go. It was like being driven by some force more powerful than herself. With an instinct that shocked her, she sent her fingers fluttering sensually down from Adam's arms to his waist. Then, unbelievably, her arms were around him and she was pressing her open hands into his back, thrusting herself against him and kissing him back with a passion that shocked them both. Adam let out a muted groan of excitement, then his mouth took fierce possession of hers in a long, probing kiss that made her throb with yearning for something more. Small, mewing cries of delight escaped her and she let her body lean temptingly against his.

'Oh, Adam!' she gasped.

She could see what effort it cost him to break away from her, but even then he did not let her go. Threading his fingers through her rain-soaked hair, he pressed her fiercely against his chest and rested his cheek on the top of her head. She could hear the frantic thudding of his heart and feel the heat coming off his body in waves.

'You should take a shower,' he urged. 'Get changed!'

With a sudden violent movement, he shook himself free of her and turned as if to go. Caroline flinched. If I had any pride at all, she thought despairingly, I'd let him go. But I love him! Of its own accord, her hand stretched out and touched his arm.

'Don't go,' she begged.

He turned back to her, his face grim and contemptuous.

'You know what's going to happen if I stay. Don't you, Caroline?' he demanded.

A tremor ran through her body, but her grey eyes remained steady. Slowly, holding her breath, she nodded.

'You're going back to London as soon as the storm is over,' he reminded her furiously. 'It would be pure insanity.'

'I know,' she agreed huskily.

'And yet you want to do it, knowing damned well that it's nothing more than a one-night stand?'

His scorn wounded her to the core. What he was offering was an insult, and yet in some strange fashion Caroline felt it was her last chance to become a real woman. No other man would ever move her, excite her, infuriate her as Adam Fletcher did, and she knew she would never take such a risk again. She could play it safe and send him away or she could accept the pain and take her chances on fulfilment. Whatever she did, she knew she was going to suffer. Yet with a deep, piercing sense of acceptance, she knew she must take that risk. It was a pity that Adam wasn't offering love, but she was old enough to know that miracles don't happen. Her mouth twisted.

'Well?' he demanded savagely. 'Is that what you want? A one-night stand?'

Caroline tossed her head.

'Yes,' she said defiantly.

He let out his breath in a low rasp.

'Then I suggest we begin by taking a shower,' he murmured. 'Together.'

His fingers hooked inside the sweetheart neckline of her T-shirt and he drew her slowly and sensually towards him. Reaching into the shower, he gave the taps a swift twist, so that a torrent of water rained down. Then with deft fingers, he seized the hem of her T-shirt and peeled it swiftly over her head. A wash of colour flooded her face as his blue eyes rested glintingly on the gentle swell of her breasts above her lacy bra.

'Oh, come now,' he taunted. 'You're not going to go all shy and virginal on me now, are you? Games are all very well, Caroline, but I think you should realise that we're not playing any more. This is for real.'

A tremor went through her as he reached behind her and briskly, almost impersonally, unfastened the hooks of her bra. Then, with a mocking smile, he held the wispy garment aloft before dropping it to the floor.

'You know, I've always rather fancied the thought of undressing you slowly and then soaping you in the shower,' he remarked conversationally. 'It'll be interesting to see whether you're as sexy as I imagined you'd be.'

Caroline went hot and cold all over at this revelation, and her eyes were full of mute appeal as Adam's hands travelled down to the waistband of her shorts. He drew the damp fabric slowly down around her hips. The shorts slid to the floor and she stood naked, confronting him.

'You know, I always rather fancied the idea of undressing you too,' she whispered, pouting at him.

She hoped to goodness he wouldn't notice how her fingers trembled as she hauled his T-shirt over his head and fumbled at the zip on his shorts. But Adam was too far gone to notice. His breath was coming in long, dragging gulps and his eyes were dark with desire. As Caroline caressed him tentatively, he gave a low, choking moan.

'You little witch,' he breathed. 'Come here, damn you.'

He dragged her under the warm, thunderous roar of the shower, and she gasped with shock and delight as he took a bar of soap and began sensually rubbing it over her skin. Spirals of excitement flared through her as his maddening, expert hands found the most sensitive and secret parts of her body.

'How do you like this?' he coaxed. 'And this? And, oh, yes, how do you like this, Caroline, darling?'

Even under the slick rain of the shower, his body was hard and tough and muscular, and he used it ruthlessly to raise her to a fever pitch of longing. Breathless and whimpering, Caroline writhed helplessly in his grasp, unable to believe the sensations that were flaring through her. At last Adam seized her hand and guided it ruthlessly to where he wanted it.

'Now touch me,' he ordered hoarsely.

Mindlessly she obeyed, letting instinct be her guide. And soon he caught her against him and buried his face in her damp, fragrant hair.

'All right, Caroline,' he muttered on a ragged, in-drawn breath. 'I can't stand any more. We've got to finish this.'

His hand groped for the tap and the warm downpour of the shower was suddenly stilled. Taking her arm, he led her out on to the tiled floor. Then he threaded his fingers through her damp hair, never taking his intent blue eyes from her face.

'You're so beautiful!' he exclaimed.

She clutched at the edge of the washbasin to steady herself as he looked at her. A strange, sweet pain filled her at the sight of his naked, aroused body. He was hard and tough and suntanned with the scars of old wounds showing white against his bronze skin and a grim expression lurking at the corners of his mouth. Not an easy man to deal with. But the only man in the world for her. And he was going to be hers—even if it was only for one night. The thought sent a groundswell of love and despair surging through her.

'What is it?' he demanded harshly. 'You're not thinking about your ex-husband again, are you?'

'No,' retorted Caroline. 'I haven't thought about Jeremy for weeks.'

With a shock she realised that it was true. Her thoughts had been so full of Adam lately that memories of Jeremy had never surfaced.

'I can't even remember properly what he looked like,' she added in surprise.

'Good,' growled Adam. 'Because it's just going to be you and me now, Caroline. Nobody else.'

An unwelcome thought crossed her mind and she stared up at him with a tormented expression.

'Adam,' she faltered, 'what about Priscilla? You're not still going to marry her, are you?'

'Don't be so ridiculous,' he replied contemptuously.

His warm hand descended on her back and he propelled her ruthlessly into the bedroom. Crossing to the huge picture window, he seized the curtains and twitched them together, shutting out the uproar of the storm outside. Then he snapped on the bedside lamp so that the room was filled with a soft apricot light.

'Come here,' he ordered, lounging back on the bed with one hand outstretched towards her.

She moved slowly like a sleepwalker, unable to take her eyes away from that lean, virile body. In the glow from the lamp, Adam looked like some wild jungle creature. He was lying propped on one elbow, radiating energy and tension like some dangerously coiled spring. It was in every plane and angle of his frame from the long, athletic legs to the powerful, muscular torso with its mat of bronze hair. Above all, it was glittering in his narrowed blue eyes and the taut, sardonic curve of his mouth as he watched her approach. His hand shot out, imprisoning her wrist.

'I want you,' he breathed.

Caroline was shaking so much that her legs would scarcely support her. Yet it was not fear that sent this strange, piercing ache through her entire body, but a desire so intense that it frightened her. Surges of molten heat seemed to be pulsing through her veins and her brain was nothing but a furious whirlwind of erotic images. Unconsciously she tossed her head so that her breasts rose with the movement and her body swayed provocatively.

'I want you too,' she murmured hoarsely.

Arching her back, she sat down on the edge of the bed next to him and touched his arm. It felt warm and rather damp. Then she leant hesitantly forward to kiss his forehead. As she did so, her breasts brushed lightly against his neck. With a low growl of impatience, Adam seized her by the shoulders and rolled with her. To her astonishment she found herself pinned beneath him while his questing lips sought the source of his torment. She gave a low, shocked gasp as he took the tip of her breast in his mouth. Spirals of electricity seemed to explode in flames through her entire body and she moaned with excitement as his tongue teased the tender bud of her nipple into a hard, aroused peak. Almost against her will, she clutched his hair and guided him so that he could repeat the same delicious torment on her other breast. As his mouth moved down over her tender flesh, she felt a remote sense of shock at the thought that she was allowing this again, even encouraging it. She had always believed her ex-husband's accusation that she was frigid—but then Jeremy had never made love to her like this. Sighing deeply, she found that her body was clenched in a wild, throbbing arousal that drove her on towards total madness.

'Touch me,' Adam hissed, seizing her fingers and guiding them.

Her first tentative caresses made him give a low groan of excitement and she felt a thrill of astonishment sweep through her. Was she really arousing the same frantic need in him as he was in her? Her whole body seemed to be on fire now, licked by invisible flames that sent her writhing against him, aching for satisfaction. But Adam took delight in prolonging her torment. His maddening, expert hands brought her again and again to the point of ecstasy, only for him to draw back deliberately and then excite her further. At last, when she was rigid and shuddering with wildly dilated eyes and parted lips, he took pity on her.

'Are you ready?' he whispered hoarsely.

She could only nod, unable to speak for the waves of passion that were pulsing through her. He took her face in his hands and stared down at her and she saw that his eyes too were dark with yearning.

'Oh, Caroline,' he muttered fervently.

And unexpectedly he planted a delicate, butterfly kiss on her cheek. That kiss was so tender, so different from his earlier, wanton caresses that it touched her to the heart. Up until now instinct had let her match Adam's healthy animal lust with her own, but now emotion came surging back to overwhelm her. She was bitterly conscious that she loved Adam and that he did not love her. And yet she wanted to make this a special and wonderful moment for both of them. But could she? Did she even know how? Doubt stabbed through her and she looked up at him with alarm in her eyes.

'What is it?' he murmured.

Her fingers moved up hesitantly to trace the outline of his jaw.

'Adam?' she said shakily. 'You won't expect too much, will you? I don't want to disappoint you...'

'Don't be ridiculous,' he growled. 'I expect everything you've got to give.'

And, crushing her against him, he took it. She had anticipated pain and was stunned when it did not happen. Her arousal was so complete that her body opened joyously to him, welcoming him in as if he were the completion of her own self. His body shifted and she felt his full weight and strength drive into her, and yet the expected tension, the agonised, stubborn resistance, did not come. Instead she felt a soaring, exhilarating need for an even closer union. Winding herself around him, she gasped his name and thrust her warm, clinging body against him, glorying in his strength and power.

'Adam. Oh, Adam,' she moaned.

He responded with a thick, choking cry that she recognised as her name. Feverishly he caught her against him, rolling wildly, initiating her into a world of delight that she had never imagined. It was like some captivating madness that held them both enthralled, plunging and grappling as they sought the ultimate release. Then with shock and disbelief, Caroline felt the first, breathtaking tremor of fulfilment begin to ripple through her. Her body threshed convulsively.

'I can't!' she gasped. 'I can't!'

'You can!' insisted Adam, and he drove violently into her.

Tremor after tremor ran through her and she cried aloud as her whole being seemed to take flight and soar. Time exploded around her and the universe was nothing but a searing explosion of coloured light. She heard Adam cry out and felt him clutch her against him, but it seemed hours before she became aware of her own laboured breathing, of her pulses thudding furiously, of the storm raging outside. A slow shudder ran through her and she looked up to see him gazing intently down at her. His hands were threaded through her hair and his breath warmed her cheek.

'What's wrong?' he asked hoarsely.

'Nothing,' she replied.

And burst into tears.

'Caroline!' His voice was full of consternation as he gathered her into his arms and held her crushed against him. 'Caroline darling. Whatever's the matter?'

She sobbed quietly in his embrace, conscious only of feeling intensely foolish. And intensely wistful. If only he could go on holding her like this! If only this meant more to him than some awful one-night stand, some meaningless, mindless opportunity to show off his sexual prowess! If only he loved her! Don't be stupid, Caroline, she told herself savagely. It wasn't about love—you knew that. Swallowing hard, she hauled herself up against the pillows and reached for the box of tissues next to the bed.

'I'm sorry,' she choked, dabbing at her eyes.

'But what's wrong? What made you cry?' he insisted in a horrified voice. 'Did I hurt you?'

'No!' she retorted swiftly. Then she summoned up a watery smile. 'I'm sorry. It's nothing. I'm just being silly.'

He stared at her suspiciously and his large hand came out and tidied a stray lock of her hair.

'Why were you afraid you'd disappoint me?' he asked abruptly.

Colour washed through her face and she pulled the covers up around her knees and huddled defensively into a ball.

'Well, you know...' she mumbled in a strained voice.

'No, I don't know. Tell me,' he urged ruthlessly.

His fingers touched her under the chin, turning her face to his.

'Well?' he insisted.

His blue eyes were totally merciless and she knew he would never give up until she told him what he wanted to know. She gave an embarrassed shrug.

'Jeremy said I was frigid,' she muttered.

There was a moment's incredulous silence. Then Adam gave a derisive hoot of laughter.

'Frigid?' he echoed. 'My God, that's rich! But you surely didn't believe him, did you?'

Her face was scarlet, her voice muffled with embarrassment. She shrank further under the covers.

'Well, it seemed to be true,' she muttered. 'I never enjoyed it with him.'

'But what about with other men?' Adam persisted. 'Did you have problems with them too?'

Caroline was silent, too tense and self-conscious to admit the truth. That there had been no other men. But Adam was as shrewd as he was persistent. He stared at her searchingly for a moment, then an incredulous look came over his face.

'There hasn't been anyone else, has there?' he demanded.

Lowering her eyes, she shook her head.

'Why not?' he asked in a baffled tone. 'Is it because you're still in love with that bastard you married?'

She shook her head again.

'No,' she said bleakly. 'I'm not in love with Jeremy. In fact, I don't think I ever was.'

Adam snorted.

'That's not what you told me before,' he reminded her bitterly. 'Every time I laid a finger on you, you started bleating about your precious Jeremy!'

'I know,' she muttered. 'I'm sorry!'

'But why?' demanded Adam. 'I always suspected you were lying to me, but why did you do it?'

Caroline made a small, helpless gesture with her hands.

'Because I was frightened!' she retorted in an exasperated voice. 'Pretty pathetic, isn't it? Twenty-eight years old and frightened of sex! Not the kind of thing you shout from the roof-tops these days, is it? I didn't think I could respond normally to a man, and in any case I wasn't interested in casual affairs. Pretending I was still pining for my ex-husband was a convenient excuse to avoid getting my fingers burnt.'

'Yet you went to bed with me today, didn't you?' he pointed out. 'Why did you do that if you're so dead set against casual affairs?'

For one insane moment, Caroline wavered on the brink of telling him the truth. Because I love you, she wanted to cry. But he was lying beside her, staring down at her with wary, searching blue eyes, and she flinched at the thought of exposing herself so rashly. Stretching herself like a cat, she fixed her gaze on the ceiling, yawned and shrugged.

'I don't know. Impulse, I suppose,' she replied carelessly.

His mouth hardened.

'I see,' he agreed evenly. 'So it's just a few sexual fireworks and then back to the bright lights of London tomorrow or the next day, is that right?'

She flinched at the contempt in his voice. But after all, wasn't that exactly what he wanted himself? A brief fling followed by a careless parting?

'Something like that,' she agreed in a brittle voice.

Adam was silent for a moment, staring at her with something more like resentment than affection in his eyes. Then slowly, almost unwillingly, his hand came out and traced a line down her cheek to her throat.

'Why don't you stay?' he suggested carelessly.

Her heart leapt and her eyes shone like diamonds. She turned to him joyfully with her arms outstretched, waiting to hear him say that he loved her. And then he ruined everything.

'After all, you don't have to be back at work for another two or three months, do you?' he added coolly. 'We could have a much more exciting fling if you stayed on a bit longer.'

CHAPTER EIGHT

CAROLINE woke the following morning to the sound of rain drumming steadily on the tin roof. At first she was startled to find Adam beside her, and then memory came hurtling back. A swift rush of colour burned her cheeks and she raised herself on one elbow to look down at him. In sleep he seemed much younger, with the harsh lines in his forehead relaxed and the tough look missing from the corners of his mouth. He had flung one arm possessively across her and she could not get out of bed without disturbing him. Not that she cared. Last night's passionate encounter had been an awesome revelation of the power of her own feelings towards Adam. Now she wanted nothing better than to gaze and gaze at him, as if she could memorise every hollow and line and angle of his body.

'I love you, Adam,' she whispered soundlessly.

And yet it was almost as if he heard her, for he came awake suddenly. For an instant he looked at her searchingly. In the half-light his eyes were dark blue and filled with an urgent, hungry yearning.

'Caroline——' he began huskily, running one finger down the outline of her jaw.

'Yes?'

He continued to look at her for a moment, as fiercely as if he were devouring her, then suddenly his face changed. His look was still warm, but no longer unguarded.

'Nothing,' he muttered. 'Nothing important.'

Pulling her down to him, he caressed her bare contours with skilful brown hands and nuzzled the softness of her cheek. When she spoke again, she could feel the vibration of his voice and the tickling warmth of his breath on her skin.

'What about your fire lily seeds?' he asked. 'Won't you have to go straight back to England to grow those?'

'Trying to get rid of me already?' she teased.

But to her dismay there was a catch in her voice.

'Don't be stupid,' retorted Adam. 'I invited you to stay, didn't I? But after all, the fire lily seeds are the whole reason why you came here. So you won't just give up on them, will you?'

'No,' Caroline admitted. 'But there's really no reason why I have to take them back to Britain myself. Your friend Patrick Edmundson in Canberra offered to help me in any way he could with the project. If I could get the seeds to him, I'm sure he could seal them in foil and airmail them to the right people in London for me.'

'Won't you need a Customs permit or anything like that?' he asked.

'No, nothing at this end. Of course they may have to go into quarantine for a while once they reach England. But my part in the project is finished now. And I'm quite certain my colleagues in London can take over from here onwards.'

Adam gave a sigh of satisfaction.

'Well, good!' he exclaimed. 'In that case, I'll open a bottle of champagne and we'll have it for breakfast.'

After they had finished the champagne and Adam had gone off to work in one of the outbuildings, Caroline took her coffee and sat in one of the huge leather armchairs near the living-room window. Although the first onslaught of the storm had abated, it was still raining outside, a heavy, drenching rain that rattled on the tin roof of the house and gurgled in the downpipes. For the first time she realised how practical the design of the house was. Built on stilts, it was too high up to flood easily and the wooden decks with their shady overhanging roofs provided plenty of outdoor living space, no matter how fierce the weather. Even if it rained for days, she thought idly, children could play quite happily out there. A wistful daydream unrolled in her head and she saw herself married to Adam with a couple of fair-haired tots playing contentedly on the deck. A pang of longing went through her at the thought. Oh, you fool, Caroline, she told herself savagely. He doesn't want you as a wife. If he were interested in marrying you, he would have asked you by now. For a moment this morning, she had suspected that Adam was on the point of making some declaration to her, but it hadn't happened. Either he had thought better of it, or it had only been her imagination at work. Yet she could have sworn that he was about to reveal his feelings to her when something had made him halt. But what? Was it the thought of Priscilla Townsend? Did he still love the other girl, in spite of his denials?

At that moment, with almost uncanny timing, the telephone rang.

'Hello,' said Caroline. 'Winnamurra Station.'

The voice on the other end was unmistakable.

'Oh, Caroline, is that you? I thought you would have been back in England by now! Well, never mind. Priscilla Townsend here. Is Adam about, please? I've got something desperately urgent to discuss with him.'

'Yes, just a moment,' said Caroline faintly, and put down the receiver with shaking fingers.

She found Adam out in the machinery shed, and when she relayed the message to him, he clicked his tongue impatiently, rose to his feet and wiped his hands on a greasy rag. His obvious reluctance to take the call cheered her a little, but her spirits soon sank again. Once inside the house, Adam disappeared into his office to take the call, spent more than half an hour talking to Priscilla and emerged whistling blithely.

In the days that followed Caroline frequently wondered whether she had gone totally insane. Too proud and too reserved to demand any explanations about Priscilla, she still suffered torments of jealousy and suspicion. And yet she could not bring herself to make a clean break in her own relationship with Adam. Nothing in her life had ever felt so ecstatically, breathtakingly right. And yet nothing had ever been so abysmally, achingly wrong. She was baffled and dismayed to find that their first, turbulent lovemaking seemed to have resolved nothing between them. There was one big change, of course. Caroline moved into Adam's room, and every night they made love with a frenzy that left her dazzled and exhausted. But there was no corresponding emotional intimacy to match their new physical closeness. And it was not until a couple of weeks after the storm that matters came to a head.

One evening Adam announced casually that his family was planning to come for a visit.

'What? When?' asked Caroline, pausing with her fork halfway to her mouth.

'Tomorrow for lunch,' he replied carelessly. 'Didn't I tell you?'

'No, you jolly well didn't!' she wailed. 'And we've no fresh vegetables. Oh, help! What can I possibly cook?'

'Now, don't flap!' drawled Adam. 'My mother is driving down from Darwin and she's sure to bring heaps of food with her. And Rosemary's coming up from Tanamingu Downs with Jim and the two kids. But it's no big deal, just a family lunch. You don't even need to cook anything really.'

All the same, Caroline spent the evening thawing frosty packages from the freezer and whizzing around with the vacuum cleaner. And the following morning she was up early, bustling around the kitchen amid the smells of roasting turkey and hot apple pie. By one o'clock the table in the dining area was a masterpiece of colourful salads, cold meats, crusty bread and gleaming glass and silverware. Caroline herself was red-faced and flustered, and she had just enough time to take a long, cool shower before the first car came jolting down the rutted driveway.

'Caroline! My mother's here!' called Adam from the living-room.

She came hurrying down the hall, pausing in front of a mirror to pat her hair into place and examine herself critically. As usual, she looked flawless. Her blue and rust-coloured dress clung to her slim form and her peaches-and-cream complexion was enhanced by a discreet touch of blusher and lipstick. She wore her pearl and crystal necklace and a faint fragrance of 'Ma Griffe' wafted around her as she moved. Yet in spite of her elegant exterior, her stomach was churning with nerves. How on earth would Adam's mother expect her to behave? After all, it wasn't as though Caroline had any clear status in the household. She wasn't even acknowledged as Adam's girlfriend, for heaven's sake! It would be amazing if there wasn't some awkwardness involved in this visit.

And yet the short, plump, grey-haired woman who was ploughing her way up the stairs didn't seem conscious of any awkwardness. She was half hidden by a massive cardboard carton, which Adam ran to take from her as she reached the deck.

'Hello, son,' she said, taking his face in her hands and kissing him on both cheeks. 'How are you?'

'Fine, thanks,' he replied, putting one arm around her and propelling her inside the house. 'How are you?'

'Couldn't be better,' answered his mother carefully, putting her bag down in a corner and looking around her. 'My word, this all looks nice. I've never seen the place so tidy.'

'That's Caroline's doing,' said Adam, setting down the carton. 'Come and meet her.'

Caroline stepped forward with her hand outstretched, only to find herself swept into the same affectionate embrace as Adam. The older woman dropped a swift kiss on her cheek, held her at arm's length and then smiled up at her with twinkling brown eyes.

'Hello, Caroline,' she said.

'How do you do, Mrs Fletcher?' murmured Caroline.

'Gwen,' insisted the older woman firmly. 'Now let me just get myself organised. Adam, this is for you. Happy birthday!'

Adam's mother was on her knees, cheerfully rummaging in the carton, so she didn't see the startled expression on Caroline's face.

'There!' she said triumphantly, handing over a package wrapped in striped red and navy paper. 'Well, go on, don't just stand there. Open it.'

But Adam scarcely seemed to see the parcel that was resting in his lean brown hands. His narrowed blue eyes were fixed warily on Caroline.

'What's the matter?' he asked.

'Why didn't you tell me it was your birthday?' she burst out. 'I haven't got a present for you or anything!'

Gwen clicked her tongue.

'Honestly!' she sympathised. 'Men are outrageous sometimes, aren't they? But please don't be offended, Caroline. He probably just didn't want you to go to any trouble over him.'

Yet Caroline saw the hostility in the look that Adam gave her and she was not convinced. He wanted to shut me out, more likely, she thought. To remind me that I'm not part of the family or the celebration and never will be. Well, damn him! Her eyes filled with angry tears, but she blinked them away and forced herself to smile.

'Yes, I'm sure you're right,' she agreed in a strained voice.

When Adam had opened his present, a new CD player, he went off to fetch them all drinks. Feeling suddenly self-conscious about her outburst, Caroline sat down and made a determined effort to be friendly.

'Have you lived in the Territory all your life, Gwen?' she asked.

'Me? Good gracious, no!' exclaimed Gwen. 'I was a city girl, born and bred in Sydney, but I met Adam's father when he was down on holidays, fell head over heels in love with him, and that was that. He was a handsome man, Jack was. A lot like Adam to look at and the same sort of nature. Knew what he wanted and nothing else would do. He proposed to me only a month after we first met, and he was so blunt I hardly even knew it was a proposal. Do you know what he said to me? He said, "Gwen, I've got to go back to the Territory next month. Are you coming with me or not?" Well, my mouth fell open. "As what?" I asked him. "Well, as my wife, of course!" he roared. "What do you think I mean, woman?" That was a fine romantic proposal now, wasn't it?'

Caroline laughed. Yet, as she saw the wistful, reminiscent look on the older woman's face, something almost like envy shot through her.

'But you accepted, didn't you?' she pointed out.

'Oh, yes,' agreed Gwen softly. 'And I never regretted it. But there were some hard times, mind you. I loathed the place when I first came here.'

'Really?' asked Caroline, startled.

'Hated it,' insisted Gwen emphatically. 'Detested it. But the trouble was that Jack's heart and soul were in the land and I knew perfectly well he'd never want to live anywhere else. Oh, I think he'd have moved if I'd asked him, but it would have destroyed him. So I stuck it out. But I think I cried every day for the first two years I was here.'

Adam returned with the drinks and stood listening with a brooding expression on his face.

'And what happened at the end of the two years?' asked Caroline with interest. 'Did you just get used to it?'

Gwen's eyes were suddenly warm and wistful.

'I had Adam,' she said simply. 'It made all the difference in the world to me.'

'Yes, I'm so wonderful that any woman could adjust to living on Mars if she had me around,' broke in Adam with heavy sarcasm. 'But the point is that you shouldn't have had to make an adjustment like that, Mum. Dad should never have asked you to do it.'

'Your father was a good man,' retorted Gwen fiercely. 'And we were very happy together. I won't hear a word against him, Adam, not even from you!'

Caroline gazed from mother to son, feeling oddly disturbed by these undercurrents of tension. But suddenly Gwen gave a robust chuckle and reached for her drink.

'Whatever will Caroline think of us, Adam?' she demanded. 'The poor girl has probably been here for weeks on end without a visitor, and now, when she finally gets one, she's treated to a family argument. We ought to be shot, the pair of us! Now, tell me, Caroline, what's all this about the fire lilies being used to make some drug?'

To her relief Caroline was able to embark on an account of her research project, and she was still describing it when the sound of another car was heard in the driveway. They all went out on to the veranda to welcome Adam's sister and her family. The two boys were absolute charmers, and Jim Cook was a lean, sun-bronzed, taciturn man, who was a perfect foil for his exuberant wife. Caroline had been a little nervous about meeting Adam's sister, but Rosemary turned out to be a tall, blonde woman of about thirty with an engaging grin and an easygoing manner. She greeted Caroline as warmly as her mother had done, kissed Adam casually and professed herself to be starving, dying of thirst and utterly driven round the twist by the long trip with the kids. However, she indicated that a large, cold drink and a decent meal would probably revive her. Before long they were all sitting around the dining table, enjoying a noisy, uproarious lunch.

All the visitors did their utmost to make Caroline feel part of the family, and yet the meal was completely spoilt for her by Adam's behaviour. Although he was ready enough to respond to Rosemary's lively chatter and teasing, he barely exchanged half a dozen words with Caroline. Whenever she spoke to him, he answered her in gruff monosyllables, and she began to feel more and more hurt and perplexed. Yet the final provocation did not come until they were lingering over coffee and fudge in the living-room. Rosemary was chatting blithely about a trip she was planning to London in the New Year and wondering where the best January sales were held, when Adam interrupted rudely.

'Why don't you ask Caroline to show you around?' he suggested harshly. 'She'll be back there by then. Her six months' leave from her job expires in January and she certainly won't stick around here once the time's up. It's all very well for a holiday, but she can't wait to get back where she belongs. The bright lights of Piccadilly are pretty damned irresistible, aren't they, Caroline?'

Caroline flushed scarlet and did not even bother to reply. She saw Rosemary and Gwen exchange troubled glances. Then Gwen cleared her throat.

'Adam,' she said evenly, 'didn't you say your prize Brahmin heifer had just had her calf? I'm sure Jim and I would both love to see it if it's somewhere nearby. Rosemary, you stay here and give Caroline a hand with the dishes.'

Within thirty seconds the room was cleared. Even the two little boys were shepherded efficiently down the stairs outside. Rosemary gave an explosive chuckle.

'Good old Mum,' she murmured. 'She's about as subtle as a bulldozer sometimes, but it gets results. Now you and I can have a chat, Caroline.'

'A chat?' echoed Caroline in an alarmed voice. 'What about?'

'About my dear brother Adam, of course. Mum knows I'm more efficient than the CIA when it comes to worming information out of people. That's why she left me here with you. So please spill the beans, Caroline, and put us out of our misery! What on earth is going on between you two?'

'Nothing,' said Caroline hastily, springing to her feet and hurrying into the dining-room. 'He made that perfectly clear, didn't he?'

Rosemary scurried after her and faced her across the table.

'No, he didn't,' she disagreed. 'The one thing he made perfectly clear to me is that he's absolutely crazy about you, Caroline.'

'That's absurd!' retorted Caroline, but tears sprang to her eyes.

She began clearing and stacking plates with nervous, jerky movements.

'Look, Caroline, I'm sorry to be such a snoop,' said Rosemary pleadingly. 'But I'm concerned about Adam. He really is an awfully nice bloke, however rude he was being today, and both Mum and I would love to see him happily married. We were thrilled to bits when we heard that you were staying here and we simply couldn't resist coming out to meet you. Well, now we have, and we can see how nice you are. And Adam's obviously head over heels in love with you, so what's the problem? Don't you love him?'

Caroline made a choking sound in the back of her throat. Then, staring sightlessly in front of her, she set two untouched slices of Black Forest gateau neatly down on a platter full of turkey.

'I didn't say that,' she retorted in a muffled voice.

'Do you love him?' demanded Rosemary bluntly.

Caroline shrugged.

'Do you?' insisted Rosemary.

'Well, how can I lie to the CIA?' retorted Caroline with brittle gaiety. 'Yes, I love him, Rosemary! But it doesn't make a blind bit of difference whether I do or not. He just doesn't want a serious relationship with me. All he wants is a lighthearted fling with no complications.'

Rosemary sat down and sighed. Then she began efficiently scraping and stacking plates.

'You're wrong, you know,' she said. 'Adam's not that kind of man, and he never has been. He wants a wife and family, and he's never made any secret of it.'

'Well, if he does, I'm not the wife he wants,' retorted Caroline moodily. 'I think he's probably still in love with that girl he nearly married.'

'Priscilla?' echoed Rosemary incredulously. 'Don't be ridiculous, Caroline. Adam knows perfectly well that would never have worked out. They were totally unsuited to each other, and when she came up here to stay it was obvious within a month that they really had nothing in common apart from the diplomatic merry-go-round. And of course, Priscilla couldn't stand Winnamurra. She said the loneliness drove her crazy. But I don't think Adam could bear to live anywhere else now.'

'No,' agreed Caroline softly, recalling how Adam had stared out over the vast, sunlit landscape when she first met him. 'And I can understand that. It really is the most amazing place, so huge, so empty, so primitive and yet so teeming with life. I'm going to miss it desperately when I leave.'

Rosemary looked startled.

'Really?' she demanded. 'But you're a Londoner. I thought you couldn't wait to get back to London.'

Caroline smiled wryly.

'That's what Adam thinks too,' she said. 'But it isn't true. I've never liked big cities much.'

'Caroline, we are a pair of idiots,' murmured Rosemary slowly. 'Don't you see that's it? That's the whole problem! Obviously Adam thinks you couldn't bear to live in the outback, and that's why he hasn't asked you to marry him!'

'That's absurd,' said Caroline doubtfully.

'Is it?' demanded Rosemary. 'Look, Caroline, Adam grew up knowing perfectly well how much our mother hated the outback. And then he got engaged to another woman who detested the place so much that she couldn't bear to marry him. Would it really be so amazing if he thought you felt the same way about it?'

Caroline bit her lip and stared uncertainly at her.

'Have you ever told Adam that you'd like to live here permanently?' demanded Rosemary.

'No,' admitted Caroline.

'Then will you give it a try?' begged Rosemary. 'Please, Caroline. I'm only asking for your own sake. And Adam's. Will you try it?'

A faint, uncertain smile began to play around the corners of Caroline's mouth. The haunted look vanished from her face and her eyes began to sparkle.

'All right,' she agreed breathlessly.

After Adam's relatives left the following morning, Caroline finally took her courage in both hands and tackled him. He was standing in the living-room staring out of the picture window as the two cars lurched away through the huge red puddles on the driveway.

Caroline came across to join him and stood looking out at the leaden sky and the strange red landscape that stretched away beyond the neat boundaries of the homestead. Her pulses were racing and there was an odd, breathless constriction in her chest. The thought of revealing her innermost longings to Adam made her feel appallingly vulnerable, but she clenched her fists and took the plunge.

'There's something I want to tell you,' she blurted out.

'What?' asked Adam sharply. 'You're not leaving, are you?'

'No,' said Caroline in a rush. 'Quite the opposite. I just want you to know that I've fallen in love with this place and I wish I could stay here forever.'

She heard his swift intake of breath, then he swung her around to face him.

'Do you mean it?' he demanded.

'Of course I mean it,' she replied with dignity.

The tortured look on his face gave way slowly to an expression of incredulous delight. Then he crushed her against him and held her so tightly that she squeaked.

'Caroline, that's the best news I ever heard in my life!' he exclaimed hoarsely.

She gazed up at him, aware that she was grinning like an idiot and that a positive sunburst of warmth seemed to be radiating through her entire body. Adam bent down and kissed her fiercely on her open mouth.

'Of course, it would be better still if you'd fallen in love with me,' he added in an injured voice.

Caroline smiled.

'Oh, I think that could be arranged,' she replied primly.

He lifted her off her feet and swung her into the air with a whoop of delight.

'It had better damned well be arranged,' he ordered. 'I don't want any woman for my wife who isn't madly in love with me!'

'W-wife?' she echoed.

'Of course. Didn't I ask you to marry me?'

'No, you did not!' retorted Caroline indignantly.

'Well, I'm asking you now,' said Adam huskily, and he let her slide slowly down until she was standing in the warm, hard circle of his arms. 'Will you marry me, Caroline?'

Caroline closed her eyes and leant blissfully against his chest, aware that she had never been happier in her life.

'Yes,' she said simply.

Adam didn't speak for a moment. He just squeezed her so hard that her ribs felt ready to crack. Then he cupped her face in his hands and gave her a long, fervent kiss.

'I love you,' he growled.

The admission seemed to be torn out of him painfully, almost against his will. Caroline's eyes fluttered open and she gazed up into his tormented face.

'You make it sound like some dreadful secret,' she protested.

'It has been,' he agreed passionately. 'I think I loved you from the very first moment I set eyes on you, but I couldn't believe you'd ever feel the same way about me. It's been pure torture having you here under my roof, loving you, wanting you and yet thinking you were going to leave at any moment.'

'Well, why didn't you tell me?' she wailed. 'I thought you wanted to get rid of me.'

'Get rid of you?' he echoed in horror. 'Whatever gave you that idea?'

Caroline's thoughts flashed back to their first meeting and Adam's tight-lipped rage.

'When I first met you, you were furious with me,' she faltered. 'I'd never met anyone so hostile before, and I couldn't understand why.'

Adam winced.

'That's true,' he admitted, letting his fingers trace the outline of her cheek. 'But I explained that to you. I kept thinking you could easily have been killed and I wanted to shake you for being so reckless. But my anger didn't last.'

'Yes, it did!' she protested. 'When we were out camping together and you almost made love to me, you were so furious I thought you'd overturn the jeep on the way home.'

'Sweetheart,' said Adam through clenched teeth, 'you'd just told me you were thinking about your husband while I touched you. Believe me, that's not the kind of news to put a man in the nicest possible temper.'

'I'm sorry,' sighed Caroline. 'Jeremy does seem to have come between us rather a lot, doesn't he?'

'He certainly does,' he agreed. 'If I hadn't known you were still in love with him, I would have spelled out my feelings for you long ago. But I wanted to give you time to get him out of your system.'

Caroline caught her breath. What a fool she had been to tell Adam such a lie! She gazed up at him regretfully.

'What is it?' he asked. 'You're *not* still in love with Jeremy, are you?'

She shook her head.

'I've told you before, I don't think I ever was,' she replied with a catch in her voice. 'I was just young and foolish and in love with the idea of being married. But Jeremy very quickly disillusioned me.'

Some bitter undertone in her voice caught Adam's attention. He looked at her sharply.

'What exactly do you mean?' he asked. 'Is it something to do with that ridiculous idea you had that you were frigid?'

'Partly,' she admitted. 'It has to do with a lot of things, Adam. Once I'd been with you for a while, I realised that I could feel passion, but I was still terribly unsure of myself. Jeremy destroyed all my self-confidence, you see.'

'What did he do to you?' he demanded in a grim voice.

Haltingly she explained about Jeremy's infidelities, his drinking habits, the way he had made her feel responsible for all the problems in their marriage.

'So it wasn't love that was holding me back,' she finished. 'It was a lot of unresolved pain.'

'My poor darling,' whispered Adam, and crushed her against him.

A wave of joy swept through her as she felt his breath stir her hair and heard the slow, rhythmic thudding of his heart. She let out a deep, luxurious sigh and snuggled closer into his embrace.

'I wish you'd told me all this before,' muttered Adam, looking down at her with fierce protectiveness. 'I would have shown you that not all men are like that.'

'Well, it's over now,' said Caroline serenely. 'I've finally managed to put the past behind me, just the way you kept urging me to do. And my future is here at Winnamurra with you.'

Adam's blue eyes clouded and he released her suddenly. Pacing across to the huge window, he lounged against it with folded arms and gazed piercingly at her.

'Are you sure?' he rasped.

Bewildered by this sudden change of mood, she stared back at him in consternation.

'Of course I'm sure!' she protested. 'I love you, Adam! Why else do you think I've been sharing your bed for these last few weeks?'

He gave a mirthless laugh.

'The two things don't necessarily go together,' he pointed out. 'You could have been sleeping with me for any number of reasons. Because you wanted to stay around near the rock paintings, because you felt like a harmless fling, because you wanted to prove that you weren't really frigid and I was a handy partner——'

'Is that what you think?' demanded Caroline in an outraged voice. 'Do you really believe this rubbish you're talking?'

He shrugged in exasperation.

'No,' he muttered. 'Although all those possibilities have occurred to me at one time or another. But what I do believe, Caroline, is this. That even though you may think you're in love with me right now, your career is going to exert a very strong pull as time goes on. After all, didn't you tell me that you were a career woman before everything else?'

She sighed.

'Yes, I did,' she admitted. 'But that wasn't the whole truth, Adam. There have been times when my career has been vitally important to me, simply because it was the only thing I had left. But even in those days I used to envy women with husbands and families. I remember riding on a bus one day and seeing a man and woman pushing a pram together and laughing. When they stopped at the traffic lights, he put his arm around her shoulders and hugged her. Such a simple thing, but it moved me almost to tears. There's never been any doubt in my mind that love means far more than any career.'

Adam still looked unconvinced.

'I don't know,' he muttered. 'I'd love to believe you, Caroline. But my mother detested this place and Priscilla did too. I'd hate to be responsible for putting you through that kind of misery.'

Caroline stiffened at the mention of Priscilla's name.

'Adam, you never did tell me what was really happening between you and Priscilla,' she murmured in a troubled voice. 'Did you really make love to her that night in Canberra?'

He seized her by the arms and gave her a playful shake.

'Of course I didn't!' he retorted. 'But when you were so jealous, I decided to keep you guessing. I thought it might jolt you into admitting that you really cared about me.'

'Oh, I cared,' she sighed. 'I cared more than I've ever cared about anyone in my life. But Priscilla's phoned you twice since we've been back from Canberra. Are you sure you're not still in love with her?'

Adam gave a muffled chuckle.

'Quite sure,' he agreed. 'It's a pity you didn't listen in to those conversations, my love. The first time she phoned to say she'd found another lover who left me for dead when it came to money, status and personal charm. And the second time she wanted to discuss the trade figures on live-meat exports to Japan. Heavy romantic stuff, I can assure you!'

Caroline giggled unwillingly.

'Well, in that case, I can't see that we have any problems,' she said.

'But are you sure you can live happily here?' he persisted. 'The Territory is a tough environment, Caroline, and a lot of women can't stand the loneliness. Of course, it's not as bad these days as it used to be, and Winnamurra Station makes a good income—damned good income. I could take you to England for a holiday once a year and you could fly to Bali or Hong Kong whenever you felt like it. And of course there'd be trips to Canberra. But there'd still be an awful lot of time when you'd be sitting around here feeling lonely.'

'Adam, I've never felt lonely here!' protested Caroline. 'I've always had you for company, and anyway, I've been far too busy with my work to notice when I was alone.'

'Yes, but your fire lily project is finished now!' he pointed out. 'And how the hell will you cope when there's no work left to do?'

'Oh, for heaven's sake!' she cried impatiently. 'I don't need to have a paid job to feel useful, if that's what you're suggesting. And, as for unpaid work, there's enough here to keep me going for several lifetimes. I mean, this place is an absolute paradise for any botanist! All right, the fire lily project may be over, but there are still thousands of plants out there which are totally unknown to science at the moment and just waiting for somebody to study them. How do we know that they won't yield wonderful drugs too? And besides, what's to stop me from setting up a fire lily plantation if they prove to be medically valuable?'

Adam shook his head admiringly.

'You seem to have it all worked out,' he admitted.

Caroline nestled against him.

'Yes, I do,' she replied pertly. 'And anyway, if all else fails, I could always try your mother's remedy for loneliness.'

He looked baffled for a moment. Then his eyes narrowed with sudden comprehension.

'Having babies?' he demanded hoarsely.

'If you want to,' said Caroline with her eyes lowered and her fingers fiddling restlessly with the buttons on his shirt.

A lean, hard finger touched her chin and raised it. Her eyelids fluttered and she gazed up into Adam's blazing blue eyes.

'Well, if you want the truth, Caroline,' he murmured throatily, 'I want to give you a baby more than anything else in the world. You can't imagine what it does to me to think of seeing your body swell with my child. I'll be the proudest man alive when that happens.'

His hands moved caressingly down over her breasts and came to rest on her belly. She could see the naked sincerity and passion in his gaze and her body pulsed with an answering heat.

'Oh, Adam,' she whispered softly. 'My love.'

He reached out to her and slowly, tauntingly began to unbutton her blouse.

'In fact,' he growled, 'I think we ought to start practising right now.'

CHAPTER NINE

ADAM'S sister Rosemary was thrilled when they telephoned to tell her of their wedding plans.

'When's it going to be?' she demanded. 'As soon as the wet season's over? What a good idea! The country will be a mass of wildflowers in May and we'll have a huge shindig to celebrate the wedding. But listen, Caroline, we can't wait that long for a decent get-together. I'll tell you what. Let me have a couple of weeks to round everybody up and I'll give you the biggest engagement party this side of Alice Springs. How's that?'

Rosemary was as good as her word, and soon all the telephones and radios in the area were humming with the news of the engagement and the coming party. A ring was delivered by mail order from a Darwin jeweller's and everything seemed to be going splendidly. Yet two days before the party Caroline did something which seemed perfectly harmless, but which almost wrecked her relationship with Adam forever.

On the Thursday morning Adam was out on the range attending a difficult calving and Caroline was at home preparing to look at some fire lily specimens. Unfortunately she couldn't find her favourite plant hand lens, and a search of the house failed to locate it anywhere. She sat down to think and after five minutes was rewarded by a sudden inspiration. Of course! She must have dropped it at the fire lily site on the day of the thunderstorm. A wave of annoyance swept over her. The lens was expensive, would be difficult to replace and would be worth nothing if it were left out in the weather for the rest of the wet season. She must get it back. But Adam had forbidden her ever to go out to the fire lily site alone and there was no hope that he could escort her. Two minutes' thought made Caroline dispose of that objection. After all, Adam trusted her now, the track was dry and clearly marked and the only possible problem was that another thunderstorm might occur without warning. She decided to ask Danny Japulula about the weather.

The dark-skinned stockman was down by the cattle-yards, branding young steers, but he left his work and came across to join her when she called him from the jeep.

'Do you think it'll rain today, Danny?' she asked.

He looked at the sky and shook his head.

'No, missus, you'll be all right,' he replied.

'Thanks. I'll see you later,' she said with a wave.

There were several destinations she could have been heading for on that track, and she did not stop to discuss her plans with Danny. When she reached the fire lily field, she spent a fruitless half-hour treading the blackened ground, but without finding her lens. Then she remembered that she and Adam had paid a quick visit to the sacred paintings before collecting the seeds. As in the past, the atmosphere under the rock overhang left her feeling awed and vaguely creepy, but her sharp eyes soon spotted her missing lens. It was lying on a heap of dried grass that had blown on to the rock floor and luckily was not damaged. She was just wiping it off when a hand descended on her shoulder. She almost jumped out of her skin.

'Danny!' she exclaimed. 'You scared the life out of me! What on earth are you doing here?'

'I came to ask you the same thing, missus,' he said, shaking his head. 'You know the boss don't like you coming out here alone.'

Caroline looked guilty.

'I know,' she admitted. 'But I lost my lens, see? And I wanted to find it again before the wet season set in. I wasn't going to harm the sacred paintings.'

'I never thought you were,' said Danny. 'But sup-
posin' you had an accident out here, eh? Or you met a
snake? Better for you to be with someone who can
protect you. Now come on, put your lens away and we'll
go back home. I bet you got lots to do before this party
on Saturday.'

On the way back to their vehicles, they chatted about
the forthcoming engagement party and Caroline's work.

'You know, our tribal elders are real proud of you,
missus,' said Danny. 'They like to think that you can
use our traditional knowledge to save people's lives. Old
Charlie Yunupingu told me yesterday that if it wasn't a
ten-day walk, he'd go all the way to Tanamingu Downs
to see you get properly betrothed to Adam.'

Caroline stopped dead, feeling overwhelmingly
touched by this.

'Oh, Danny!' she exclaimed. 'I'm so sorry. It never
occurred to me to invite the tribal elders to our party,
because they move around such a lot. But we'd love to
have them if they'd come. Do you think they'd be prepared to ride in a bus, or would that be too modern for
them?'

'I reckon they'd give it a go for you and Adam,' said
Danny, grinning.

So it was that on the morning of the engagement party,
the entire population of Winnamurra set out in a collection of buses, cars and jeeps to drive the two hundred
miles south to Tanamingu Downs. Caroline and Adam
had a jeep to themselves, but every other vehicle was
packed to capacity with well-wishers. Although the wet
season was now well under way, the rain held off for the
day and they encountered little flooding. With the
moisture from the recent rains, much of the country was
already turning lush and green and steamy. The vast
flood plains with their teeming bird life and exotic plants
gave Caroline a sense of exhilaration that she had never
known in more urbanised areas of the world.

'It's so wild,' she explained to Adam. 'So untouched. It makes me feel as if I'm one of the first humans on earth—or one of the last.'

'That's right,' he agreed with satisfaction, reaching out to pat her on the leg. 'I'm glad you understand. It makes me feel that way too. Mind you, if I know Rosemary, you won't feel like that once we reach Tanamingu. I reckon she'll have everyone from five hundred miles away over for the party.'

Adam was right. In spite of living in splendid isolation, Rosemary had managed to rustle up over a hundred people to attend the party. Neighbours had come by car, by jeep and even by helicopter to celebrate the engagement. There were few people that Caroline herself knew. Adam's mother and his brother Bruce had travelled down from Darwin, Mark Sloane and his wife had flown in from Queensland, the Webbs had driven down and a bus had been hired to transport the Aborigines from Winnamurra Station. Apart from these, all the other guests were strangers, but full of the casual friendliness that was typical of Australians. The entertainment was rough and ready but extremely lavish. Two whole steers were barbecued on spits and there were uncountable sausages, hamburgers and sizzling bacon rashers. A large marquee had been set up to hold the vast trestle-tables filled with salads and cakes and tropical fruit, and in the shade of a huge peppercorn tree half a dozen volunteer barmen were doing a brisk trade with barrels of cold beer and crates of soft drink. Since most of the guests had travelled so far, it was taken for granted that everyone would stay overnight, and when darkness fell, there was a huge bonfire with fireworks for the children, followed by a bush dance for the adults. Caroline enjoyed herself hugely.

By noon the following day most of the guests had melted away. Caroline and Adam stayed on for a leisurely lunch, but Adam kept glancing doubtfully at the sky.

'I think we're in for more rain by tonight,' he said.

'Well, you've always been the best weather prophet in the family,' said Rosemary. 'So I suppose you two had better be on your way. But keep in touch, won't you, Caroline? And remember, I'm driving up to Darwin next month to do some Christmas shopping, so you'd better come with me and help me out. Now, do you want to take some of this leftover food with you? It might save you cooking for the next five years!'

The drive home was uneventful and it was close to dark when they reached Winnamurra. Caroline was floating in a mood of dreamy contentment, but as they began climbing the stairs towards the house, the lean, dark figure of Danny Japulula appeared on the veranda above them. His usual smile was missing and his face was so serious that a pang of foreboding went through her. Obviously Adam felt the same way, for his voice was sharp with alarm as he addressed his foreman.

'Danny! What is it, mate? Has something happened?'

'Too bloody right it has,' agreed Danny. 'That Michael Barclay feller's been back and stolen the rest of the sacred paintings.'

'*What*?' Adam stood riveted to the spot with horror, his hand clutching the railing. 'But how? When?' he demanded. 'How the hell did he manage it?'

Danny shrugged glumly.

'Easiest thing in the world, mate,' he replied. 'We were all down the road at your binge and he just sneaked in while the place was deserted. When I got home, I saw fresh four-wheel-drive tracks leading down past the stockyards and I smelt a rat right away. I drove down in the jeep, but Barclay's been too flamin' clever for us this time. The whole painting's been cut away.'

'Well, he'll regret it!' vowed Adam in a dangerous voice. 'I'm going to catch him if it's the last thing I do!'

'I dunno, mate,' said Danny doubtfully. 'The police don't seem real hopeful. But they did ask me for the photos of the paintings that you took a couple of years back after the first robbery. That's what I was looking for in the house.'

'Did you find them?' demanded Adam.

Wordlessly Danny held up a small orange folder of snapshots.

'I reckon I'll go down and wait for the police to arrive,' he muttered. 'See you, Adam. See you, Caroline.'

Caroline watched in shocked silence as Danny padded miserably down the stairs. Although the paintings could never have the same spiritual significance for her as they had for the Aborigines, she was horrified by the theft. All her pleasure in the engagement party ebbed away. Tramping miserably up the rest of the stairs, she flung open the front door and snapped on the light. Then she pulled the curtains shut and stared unhappily at Adam.

'Isn't that unspeakable?' she demanded. 'I just hope they catch that rotten Michael Barclay!'

'Do you?' asked Adam in an odd voice.

'Well, of course I do!' she retorted heatedly. 'Whatever do you mean?'

Adam's face might have been carved out of granite. His mobile mouth was set in a sneer and his blue eyes were cold and hostile.

'Just this!' he said through clenched teeth. 'It seems remarkably convenient that Michael Barclay was able to sneak in and steal everything while every last inhabitant of the place was away at your engagement party, doesn't it, Caroline? Especially when it was your kind and generous idea to hire the bus to take all the Aboriginal families down there?'

Caroline stared at him in horror. She felt as if a yawning abyss had opened under her feet.

'W-what do you mean?' she faltered.

'Isn't it obvious?' he retorted. 'You planned this whole thing, didn't you? That was a real stroke of genius, luring everyone two hundred miles away so your old friend Barclay could steal the rest of the paintings! I've got to hand it to you, Caroline—you're imaginative.'

'Not half so imaginative as you!' she whipped back. 'You must be crazy if you believe this rubbish, Adam!'

'Oh, no,' he growled in a low, dangerous voice. 'Not any more, Caroline. I'll admit I was crazy for a while, crazy enough to believe that you loved me. But not any more. I can see what you are now.'

Caroline's heart was thudding so furiously that she felt the blood pumping in swift, angry waves into every corner of her body. A great rush of adrenalin swept through her, making her voice shake with rage and disbelief.

'And what am I?' she demanded in a hoarse whisper.

'A heartless, scheming little whore, who doesn't care who she sleeps with just to get what she wants.'

'How dare you?' she choked. 'Well, if that's what you think of me, Adam, you can have your ring back! I'm not marrying a man who can hold that sort of opinion of me!'

With a deep, rending sob of anger and grief, she twisted the ring off her finger and hurled it at him. It struck him in the chest and rebounded on to the floor, but he did not even bother to glance down at it. His smouldering blue eyes were fixed unwinkingly on Caroline. Raising his hands, he gave three slow, insulting claps.

'Nice performance!' he taunted. 'I love the quivering lip, sweetheart. And it saves time throwing the ring at me now, doesn't it? Otherwise we'd have to have another pathetic little scene two weeks down the track, wouldn't we? The one where you tell me you've made a mistake and you're not in love with me after all?'

'You swine!' breathed Caroline.

Adam took a step closer, his eyes still fixed glitteringly on hers. There was something indefinably menacing in that tall, powerful figure.

'Tell me,' he said silkily, 'do you sleep with Barclay too? Well, of course you do! After all, you sleep with perfect strangers, so you'd hardly refuse your old buddy in crime, would you? But does he turn you on, Caroline? How do I compare with him in the sack?'

Caroline pressed the back of her fist to her mouth and gazed at him out of wide, frightened grey eyes. This was a nightmare, it couldn't possibly be happening, this couldn't be Adam staring down at her with such blazing hatred in his gaze!

'Stop it!' she begged in a muffled voice.

Adam pulled her hand roughly away from her mouth.

'Why?' he demanded ruthlessly. 'Why should I take any pity on you? I loved you, Caroline! But you didn't have any pity on me, did you? I could forgive you everything else, but to come into my bed like that, to pretend that you loved me . . . ! Still, there are some things that are impossible to fake, and desire is one of them. And at least I have the satisfaction of knowing that you wanted me, Caroline, however much you fought against it!'

His eyes were smoky with rage and with something else that set off alarm bells in her brain. She tried to pull away, but found herself caught up short in that merciless grip.

'Don't flatter yourself!' she cried wildly, fighting down a rising panic. 'I never wanted you, Adam! Never!'

'You're lying!' he snarled. 'Your own body betrays you. I could always tell when you wanted me, Caroline, and I know you want me even now.'

'That's not true!' she raged.

'Isn't it?' he murmured hoarsely. 'Well, why don't we find out?'

With a swift, pitiless movement he imprisoned her chin in his hand and then his lips came down on hers. It was the most brutal kiss Caroline had ever suffered in her life. Adam's tongue thrust fiercely into her mouth and he kissed her as if he wanted to devour her. Gasping in protest, she tried to fight her way free, only to find her head being tugged ruthlessly back into position. In a shameless display of raw, masculine arrogance, Adam held her captive, plundering her mouth with his and hauling her slim body frenziedly against him. At first Caroline fought him, but her struggles only seemed to excite him further, so she changed her tactics and let her body go limp in his arms.

But it was a fatal mistake, for he was totally merciless when it came to pressing his advantage. The moment she lowered her guard, his hands thrust urgently inside her dress and began tormenting her tender breasts. She let out a whimper of protest that was halfway to being a whimper of excitement. Adam uttered a low, throaty growl of triumph and very slowly and sensually traced a whorl on her nipple. Caroline cried out at the sudden pressure of his thumb, but a treacherous ripple of longing went through her, making her shudder.

'You want me, don't you?' he breathed against her ear.

'No!' she gasped, trying desperately to drag his hands away from her bodice. 'Don't be ridiculous!'

But her body and her mind seemed to be operating on two different wavelengths. And, in spite of her protests, her eyes were dark and soft with burgeoning desire. When he caught her fiercely against him once more, she did not resist, but kissed him back with an angry, ravenous sensuality. Gasping with hostility and passion, he drew her down to the floor and pushed her relentlessly back on to a rawhide rug. His powerful thighs were around her, imprisoning her slender body, and his massive work-hardened shoulders loomed threateningly above her.

'Just one more farewell bout?' he taunted. 'What do you say, sweetheart?'

Then his hands reached up under her skirt and stripped off her bikini pants. Her breathing came in shallow, rapid flutters as she lay eyeing him watchfully. A complete maelstrom of emotions surged through her—rage, humiliation, passion, hate. But she did not try to prevent him as he slowly unbuckled his belt and kicked off his Levi jeans.

He took her with a force and savagery that appalled her. And yet, even in that loveless coupling, some spark of ecstasy overtook her, sending them both hurtling over the edge into a new dimension of fulfilment. Afterwards they lay together, spent and shuddering, but Adam did not even murmur her name. Instead, he dragged himself clear of her, rose to his feet and stood staring down at her, naked and menacing.

'Now get out,' he ordered.

A month later Caroline stood looking out of a window at the grey streetscape of London. It was only four o'clock, but already it was nearly dark. Snow was falling silently in the empty playground far below her and the trees that lined the Thames embankment were black and leafless. On her way home she had seen a group of carol-singers going from door to door with a lantern, and somewhere far off she could hear the sweet, piercing notes of 'Hark, the Herald Angels Sing!' I hope they don't come here! she thought savagely. I don't feel up to Christmas cheer at the moment. Or anything else, for that matter.

A wave of misery swept through her as she stared out at the gathering darkness. Unbidden memories came surging back of a harsh landscape where the light was so bright that it hurt the eyes and the sky was a vivid, dazzling blue. And there were other memories too, crueller memories of a tough, bronzed man who had made her blaze with joy and grief. But now that was all in the past and there was nothing left but a dismal future.

She heard footsteps on the stairs, and with an impatient sigh, she plodded across to open the door.

'Wretched carol-singers!' she muttered. 'I wish they'd... Oh! Oh, my goodness!'

For it was not the carol-singers who stood there, but a memory from the past. A memory that made her clutch at the door frame and stare in disbelief. A tall, blond man with a bunch of red roses in his hands and a look of anguish in his vivid blue eyes.

'Adam!' she croaked.

He took a step forward so that he was standing under the outside light and her brain registered numbly that there was snow on his coat and dark shadows under his eyes.

'May I come in?' he asked.

'No!' she cried, trying to slam the door in his face. 'No! I don't want to see you ever again!'

But he stuck his foot in the door.

'Caroline, please!' he begged. 'I've come twelve thousand miles to apologise to you. At least listen to me!'

She contemplated making a break for the stairs and rushing wildly into the night. But at that moment half a dozen red-cheeked children trooped on to the landing, shuffled nervously together and began to sing. And Adam took advantage of the diversion to step boldly inside the front door of the flat. All the time that she was listening to 'Silent Night', Caroline was thinking wildly, This can't be happening, it simply can't be happening! Yet when the singing came to an end, Adam stuffed a ten-pound note into the children's tin and closed the door behind them. And Caroline realised with a sinking sensation that she really was confronting the truth.

'How did you find me?' she whispered.

'I phoned the museum. They said you were minding this flat for a friend.'

Caroline's breath caught in her throat.

'Go away!' she begged.

'Not until you've heard me out,' said Adam firmly.

Setting down the roses on her hall table, he took a step towards her and smoothed her brown hair away from her face. For a long moment, they simply stared agonisedly at each other. Then Caroline took a rigid, shuddering breath.

'Go on,' she said hoarsely.

'What can I say?' demanded Adam. 'It all seems too glib and too obvious. But I'm sorry, Caroline, desperately, desperately sorry that I ever suspected you of plotting to steal the paintings. And I'm even more sorry for what I did to you afterwards. I was brutal—there's no other word for it.'

Caroline's fragile composure vanished.

'Yes, you were!' she flared. 'You used me as if I meant nothing to you—absolutely nothing!'

Her voice caught on a frantic sob, and Adam drew her into his arms and held her fiercely against him. Resting his cheek on her hair, he sighed heavily.

'Whereas the truth is that you mean more to me than life itself,' he muttered. 'Oh, Caroline, Caroline, I'm so sorry I ever suspected you.'

'But how could you?' she demanded, turning her tear-stained face up to his. 'What ever made you think I'd do such a thing?'

'I must have been crazy,' he admitted, wincing. 'When I realised you'd been out to the sacred site alone that day, it just began to eat me up with doubt.'

'How did you know?' she asked. 'Did Danny tell you?'

'Danny? Not exactly. I'd had closed circuit cameras and a burglar alarm installed among the rocks to film anyone who came near the place. Danny switched off the alarm, but you were both on film. It was the same method that allowed the police to catch up with Michael Barclay in the end.'

'They've caught him?' echoed Caroline, momentarily diverted.

'Yes. The alarm went off at the police station in Darwin while we were all at the party, and they picked him up at the airport a few days later and retrieved the paintings. He also admitted that you were innocent, but that's not the point. The point is that I should never have thought any different.'

'Then why did you?' she demanded.

Adam gritted his teeth.

'Perhaps because I could never believe that you were genuinely in love with me,' he said bleakly.

Caroline was silent for a moment, turning that over.

'But I was,' she whispered.

He put his finger under her chin and tilted her face up to his.

'Was?' he prompted softly.

Her heart beat violently, and it was a good thing that his arms were around her so firmly, for her legs were trembling so much that she might have fallen.

'Am,' she breathed, surrendering at last.

'That's all I needed to know,' murmured Adam.

And his mouth came down on hers in a kiss that left her no doubts at all.

Take 4 bestselling love stories FREE

Plus get a FREE surprise gift!

Special Limited-time Offer

Mail to Harlequin Reader Service®

3010 Walden Avenue
P.O. Box 1867
Buffalo, N.Y. 14269-1867

YES! Please send me 4 free Harlequin Presents® novels and my free surprise gift. Then send me 6 brand-new novels every month, which I will receive months before they appear in bookstores. Bill me at the low price of $2.49 each plus 25¢ delivery and applicable sales tax, if any*. That's the complete price and—compared to the cover prices of $2.99 each—quite a bargain! I understand that accepting the books and gift places me under no obligation ever to buy any books. I can always return a shipment and cancel at any time. Even if I never buy another book from Harlequin, the 4 free books and the surprise gift are mine to keep forever.

106 BPA ANGA

Name	(PLEASE PRINT)	
Address	Apt. No.	
City	State	Zip

POSTCARDS FROM EUROPE

HARLEQUIN PRESENTS®

Travel across Europe in 1996 with Harlequin Presents. Collect a new Postcards From Europe title each month!

Don't miss
MASK OF DECEPTION
by Sara Wood
Harlequin Presents #1628

Available in February wherever Harlequin Presents books are sold.

HPPFE2

Hi—
It's carnival time in Italy! The streets of Venice are filled with music—the costumes are incredible. And I can't wait to tell you about Lucenzo Salviati...
Love, Meredith

HARLEQUIN®

Don't miss these Harlequin favorites by some of our most distin-
guished authors!
And now, you can receive a discount by ordering two or more titles!

HT#25409	THE NIGHT IN SHINING ARMOR by JoAnn Ross	$2.99	☐
HT#25471	LOVESTORM by JoAnn Ross	$2.99	☐
HP#11463	THE WEDDING by Emma Darcy	$2.89	☐
HP#11592	THE LAST GRAND PASSION by Emma Darcy	$2.99	☐
HR#03188	DOUBLY DELICIOUS by Emma Goldrick	$2.89	☐
HR#03248	SAFE IN MY HEART by Leigh Michaels	$2.89	☐
HS#70464	CHILDREN OF THE HEART by Sally Garrett	$3.25	☐
HS#70524	STRING OF MIRACLES by Sally Garrett	$3.39	☐
HS#70500	THE SILENCE OF MIDNIGHT by Karen Young	$3.39	☐
HI#22178	SCHOOL FOR SPIES by Vickie York	$2.79	☐
HI#22212	DANGEROUS VINTAGE by Laura Pender	$2.89	☐
HI#22219	TORCH JOB by Patricia Rosemoor	$2.89	☐
HAR#16459	MACKENZIE'S BABY by Anne McAllister	$3.39	☐
HAR#16466	A COWBOY FOR CHRISTMAS by Anne McAllister	$3.39	☐
HAR#16462	THE PIRATE AND HIS LADY by Margaret St. George	$3.39	☐
HAR#16477	THE LAST REAL MAN by Rebecca Flanders	$3.39	☐
HH#28704	A CORNER OF HEAVEN by Theresa Michaels	$3.99	☐
HH#28707	LIGHT ON THE MOUNTAIN by Maura Seger	$3.99	☐

Harlequin Promotional Titles

#83247	YESTERDAY COMES TOMORROW by Rebecca Flanders	$4.99	☐
#83257	MY VALENTINE 1993	$4.99	☐
	(short-story collection featuring Anne Stuart, Judith Arnold, Anne McAllister, Linda Randall Wisdom)		

(limited quantities available on certain titles)

	AMOUNT	$
DEDUCT:	**10% DISCOUNT FOR 2+ BOOKS**	$
ADD:	**POSTAGE & HANDLING**	$
	($1.00 for one book, 50¢ for each additional)	
	APPLICABLE TAXES*	$ _____
	TOTAL PAYABLE	$ _____
	(check or money order—please do not send cash)	

To order, complete this form and send it, along with a check or money order for the
total above, payable to Harlequin Books, to: **In the U.S.:** 3010 Walden Avenue,
P.O. Box 9047, Buffalo, NY 14269-9047; **In Canada:** P.O. Box 613, Fort Erie, Ontario,
L2A 5X3.

Name: _____

Address: _____ City: _____

State/Prov.: _____ Zip/Postal Code: _____

*New York residents remit applicable sales taxes.
Canadian residents remit applicable GST and provincial taxes.

HBACK-JM

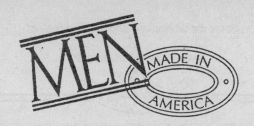

MEN MADE IN AMERICA

**Fifty red-blooded, white-hot, true-blue hunks
from every State in the Union!**

Look for MEN MADE IN AMERICA! Written by some
of our most poplar authors, these stories feature fifty of
the strongest, sexiest men, each from a different state in
the union!

Two titles available every other month at your favorite
retail outlet.

In January, look for:

DREAM COME TRUE by Ann Major (Florida)
WAY OF THE WILLOW by Linda Shaw (Georgia)

In March, look for:

TANGLED LIES by Anne Stuart (Hawaii)
ROGUE'S VALLEY by Kathleen Creighton (Idaho)

You won't be able to resist MEN MADE IN AMERICA!

Share the adventure—and the romance—of

HARLEQUIN PRESENTS®

A Year
DOWN UNDER

If you missed any titles in this miniseries,
here's your chance to order them:

Harlequin Presents®—A Year Down Under

#11519	HEART OF THE OUTBACK by Emma Darcy	$2.89	☐
#11527	NO GENTLE SEDUCTION by Helen Bianchin	$2.89	☐
#11537	THE GOLDEN MASK by Robyn Donald	$2.89	☐
#11546	A DANGEROUS LOVER by Lindsay Armstrong	$2.89	☐
#11554	SECRET ADMIRER by Susan Napier	$2.89	☐
#11562	OUTBACK MAN by Miranda Lee	$2.99	☐
#11570	NO RISKS, NO PRIZES by Emma Darcy	$2.99	☐
#11577	THE STONE PRINCESS by Robyn Donald	$2.99	☐
#11586	AND THEN CAME MORNING by Daphne Clair	$2.99	☐
#11595	WINTER OF DREAMS by Susan Napier	$2.99	☐
#11601	RELUCTANT CAPTIVE by Helen Bianchin	$2.99	☐
#11611	SUCH DARK MAGIC by Robyn Donald	$2.99	☐

(limited quantities available on certain titles)

TOTAL AMOUNT	$
POSTAGE & HANDLING	$
($1.00 for one book, 50¢ for each additional)	
APPLICABLE TAXES*	$ _____
TOTAL PAYABLE	$ _____
(check or money order—please do not send cash)	

To order, complete this form and send it, along with a check or money order for the total above, payable to Harlequin Books, to: *In the U.S.*: 3010 Walden Avenue, P.O. Box 9047, Buffalo, NY 14269-9047; *In Canada*: P.O. Box 613, Fort Erie, Ontario, L2A 5X3.

Name: _____

Address: _____ City: _____

State/Prov.: _____ Zip/Postal Code: _____

*New York residents remit applicable sales taxes.
Canadian residents remit applicable GST and provincial taxes.   YDUF